Had a woman been murdered because she resembled Eden?

Eden trembled. Instinctively she knew it was true. Cold seeped from her pores, chilling every inch of her. *She* was meant to have died tonight—with David framed for her murder.

The hotel suite she shared with David no longer seemed like an elegant love nest. Now it was like an expensive prison.

The stalker's obsession had taken a macabre turn from fixated love to hatred. Only one question remained: Would Eden be the next victim?

ABOUT THE AUTHOR

Eden's Baby is talented Adrianne Lee's third book for Harlequin Intrigue. When asked about why she wanted to write romance fiction, Adrianne had this to say: "I wanted to be Doris Day when I grew up. You know, singing my way through one wonderful romance after another. And I did. I fell in love with and married my high school sweetheart and became the mother of three beautiful daughters. Family and love are very important to me and I hope you enjoy the way I weave them through my stories. I love hearing from readers." If you want a response or an autographed bookmark from Adrianne Lee, please send an SASE to P.O. Box 3838, Sequim, WA 98382

Books by Adrianne Lee

HARLEQUIN INTRIGUE
296—SOMETHING BORROWED, SOMETHING BLUE
354—MIDNIGHT COWBOY

Don't miss any of our special offers. Write to us at the following address for information on our newest releases.

Harlequin Reader Service
U.S.: 3010 Walden Ave., P.O. Box 1325, Buffalo, NY 14269
Canadian: P.O. Box 609, Fort Erie, Ont. L2A 5X3

Eden's Baby
Adrianne Lee

Harlequin Books

TORONTO • NEW YORK • LONDON
AMSTERDAM • PARIS • SYDNEY • HAMBURG
STOCKHOLM • ATHENS • TOKYO • MILAN
MADRID • WARSAW • BUDAPEST • AUCKLAND

In loving memory of Arnie and Kate.

Special thanks to: Clint Cresawn, Ruth Craven, Sheila Keener and Stephanie K. Steppe of University of Washington Medical Center; Miriam S. Cressman of Virginia Mason Medical Center; Captain Ron Brothers of the Issaquah Police.

ISBN 0-373-22383-8

EDEN'S BABY

Copyright © 1996 by Adrianne Lee Undsderfer

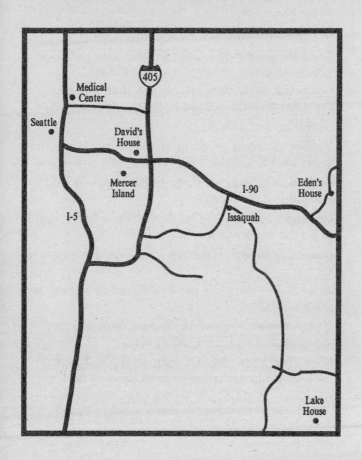

CAST OF CHARACTERS

Eden Prescott—The woman was torn between love and duty.

David Coulter—Was the handsome psychologist an object of obsessive love or a cold-blooded killer?

Valerie Prescott—Eden's sister-in-law wore her heart on her sleeve.

Beth Montgomery—Eden's sister was in a life-and-death situation.

Colleen MacLaine—Did David's secretary want to be the only woman in his life?

Denise Smalley—Did she love David enough to kill her own sister?

Ariel Bell—Was this private nurse as caring as she seemed?

Lynzy Anders—David's student aide seemed too guileless to be anything else.

Rose Hatcher—David's former student was serving a life sentence in prison.

Detective Kollecki—Was he after the truth or bent on being right?

Prologue

Life imprisonment. Dr. David Coulter felt no sense of justice as he watched from the back of the Seattle courtroom. Rose Hatcher, wearing an abnormally bland dress, her carrot red hair hanging to her waist in a limp braid, stood as the verdict was read.

David swallowed his disgust. Rose could spend eternity in jail. It wouldn't bring back Marianne DePaul, his most promising psychiatry student in years. Wouldn't console her family.

Or ease his guilt.

How could he come to terms with the knowledge that someone's obsession with him had led to the death of an innocent young woman? He jammed his trembling hands into the pockets of his jacket, unable to shake the certainty that Marianne's murder was preordained, her fate sealed, the moment he'd shown a special interest in her. Singled her out in class.

Rage boiled inside him, rage against the woman being sentenced, a rage to take her life as she'd taken Marianne's, a rage that defiled everything he had ever believed in.

He wheeled around and left the courtroom. Why hadn't he realized Rose's affection for him bordered on psychotic? His throat constricted. This was the second time he'd wrongly diagnosed someone—been tricked into taking things at face value. The first time had only humiliated him, left him distrustful of his professional and personal abilities to assess patients' and friends' motives.

This time someone innocent had died.

How could he have misjudged her so badly? He stepped aboard the elevator and punched the button with the force of his anger. His license should be revoked. He'd taken Rose's affection as transference dependency, a "crush" that patients, and sometimes students, developed for their doctors or teachers. A daily hazard to psychiatrists.

The elevator stopped, and an elderly couple boarded. Why hadn't he suspected the truth—that Rose had an antisocial personality disorder? He let out a ragged breath. At least there was no doubt of her guilt. Not only had they found physical evidence in her apartment—some of it personal items stolen from his house—but Rose had also confessed.

A clammy chill swept him. *Feel it, David. All of it. All the pain and anger. Acceptance was at the other end of this nightmarish tunnel.* How many times had he told his patients that? What worthless advice! Would acceptance ease his guilt? Restore his trust in his own judgment of people?

He stepped from the elevator and started across the lobby. It would certainly not reassure his secretary, his dentist's receptionist, his new student assistant, an ex-patient and an old girlfriend, all of whose names were on an apparent hit list investigators had found in Rose Hatcher's apartment. He shuddered to think they might all have been intended future victims because of their association with *him*.

He left the King County Courthouse, emerging into the crisp February afternoon. Exhaust smoke fouled the air, but David hardly noticed the vehicles moving along the street as he joined the few pedestrians sharing the sidewalk. He crossed Fourth Avenue and headed up the hill to the parking lot.

At the next corner, he encountered a street vendor selling flowers.

The man poked a flower in his direction. "Last chance to remember your Valentine."

A familiar fragrance reached David, freezing him in place and unsettling his stomach. His gaze riveted on the single white rose the man held toward him. It was just like the one Rose had left on his doorstep after killing Marianne.

Chapter One

Five months later

A rare July thunderstorm battered David Coulter's Mercer Island home as he set the telephone receiver back in its cradle. An open bottle of wine was breathing on the counter, and salad and steaks waited in the fridge. He'd planned on sharing dinner with an old friend. It seemed she'd gotten a better offer.

Good for her.

Bad for him.

"At least Shannon won't be lonely tonight." He wished he could find someone to share *his* life with. Friends were nice, but their company only eased the emptiness inside him; he needed someone to fill it. A vision of Eden Prescott flashed into his mind, and he pondered the tender glances they'd exchanged lately. Had he imagined a longing in her eyes? He shook his head at his foolishness. Eden was the most loyal woman he'd ever met—and her loyalties belonged to her husband.

Even if she felt as he felt about her, she'd never act on those feelings.

Wind seemed to steal into the old house, brushing a chill over his naked body. Banishing Eden from his thoughts, David hurried back to the warm bathroom, snatched up a small towel, wiped steam off the mirror, then draped the towel around his neck.

His damp hair stood on end, and the shadow of a beard darkened his jawline. He reached for his comb. It was gone. *Not another one.* He groaned. How many did that make in the last two months? Three? A shiver skittered along his spine. If Rose Hatcher weren't still behind bars...

"Whoa, old man. Talk about classic paranoia." He chuckled at himself. No obsessed students were getting in here and taking his combs. He lathered his face and shaved. More likely he'd simply set a comb down somewhere, then gotten busy with something else and forgotten where he'd put it. It would turn up where least expected. Probably in the fridge.

The doorbell rang, its merry chime chasing off the concern. Who the hell could that be? He grabbed his robe off the hook on the bathroom door, struggled into it and cinched the belt as he hurried to the foyer. He peered through the peephole.

In the eerie yellow glow cast by the porch light, he saw a bedraggled and wet-looking woman, petite in stature, her short black hair plastered to her head. His heart jumped. "Eden."

He yanked the door open, oblivious to the fact that he wore nothing more than his short terry-cloth robe, that his cocoa brown hair was damp and mussed and that a towel still draped his neck and a dab of shaving cream adorned one earlobe.

"Hello, David."

Her husky voice held him rooted in place, eliciting an unbidden, decidedly warm stirring in his belly. His mouth was suddenly as dry as the night was wet. "Eden?"

Her cornflower blue eyes widened as she took in his appearance. "I've caught you at a bad time."

"No, you haven't, but what are you doing out in this storm?" David kept her standing outside, his manners lost in the surprise of finding her on his doorstep. He noticed the mascara smudges underscoring her eyes. Had she been crying? Had something happened to her sister? "Is it Beth?"

"Well . . . no. Maybe." She looked confused, desperate, about to bolt. "I—I have no right to barge in on you. I—I should have called."

"Nonsense." She wasn't even wearing a coat or boots. Had no umbrella. Water dripped from the tips of her hair. Something was damned wrong. "Please, come in."

Her hand was icy cold and wet as he caught it and gently, firmly, pulled her inside and led her into the living room to the marble fireplace, where a roaring fire burned.

The miniblinds were closed against the storm, but the downpour drummed overhead, muffling the soft sounds of classical music issuing from the stereo against the far wall.

The room was massive, in perfect proportion to the house, and offered a grand view of Lake Washington when the blinds were open. But other than the stereo, the only furniture was a creamy leather sofa centered near the hearth with a single brass floor lamp at its side.

He saw Eden frown and assumed she was wondering at the lack of personal items. Not wanting to discuss that, he said, "I'll get you a towel."

"Thank you." She stepped out of red flats that looked as if she'd waded through a puddle, and hunched toward the flames, chafing her hands together. "I am rather chilled."

David hastened to the linen closet and grabbed a thick blue towel that was almost as large as Eden, then veered into the kitchen and filled two glasses from the open wine bottle. Eden was shaken. Maybe in shock. Whatever had brought her here could just as easily send her back out into the night. He'd seen the misgivings in her eyes, in her hesitancy at coming inside. The last thing she needed was to tear back out into this storm.

But she might.

He hurried back to the living room, breathing a sigh of relief the moment he saw her still standing at the fireplace. Thunder rumbled overhead. David slowed his step and let his gaze roam from Eden's sleek raven hair, to the delicate paleness of her neck, over every petite curve, past the shapely arch of her calves, to her graceful bare feet. A tightness jabbed his groin and made him suddenly aware of his lack of clothing.

She spun around, and their gazes met and held. "Peter has filed for divorce."

Peter was her husband. Whatever David had expected, it wasn't this. He'd been certain it was Beth. His patient. The link that had brought them together months ago. Although they'd grown friendly during their association, Eden seldom mentioned her marriage. "I'm sorry. I can see it has shaken you."

"Oh, yes. And I really need to talk to someone about it. Was I wrong to come here?"

"No, of course not." Dear God, he should have said yes. How could he bear to hear her despair over her husband? How could he control feelings for her that defied anything he'd ever felt for other women?

The thought was like a cold splash of reality. Even if what he felt for Eden was the genuine, once-in-a-lifetime thing, he had no right to act on it. She was destroyed by the failure of her marriage. She loved another.

"Here. Some cabernet will help warm your insides." He handed her the towel and one of the wineglasses. "Would you like to sit on the sofa?"

"No. I'd rather stay by the fire."

"Sure." He remained standing also, keeping a good three feet between them, terrified that the least encouragement from her would shred his already shaky professional detachment, that he would reach out to help her and be lost in the need she exuded, in the need coursing his own veins.

Be strong, be strong, he chanted silently, painfully. "What happened?"

"It seems my... husband has found someone else he wants to marry."

Oddly there was no pain in her eyes, just anger and fear. What did that mean? "I'm sorry."

The words felt so inadequate.

"Don't be." She gazed into his eyes. "The marriage was over long ago."

David felt the invisible, intangible, irresistible allure of her emotional and physical hunger... for him?

"It was?" He swallowed hard. No. He was misreading her. She didn't want him as he wanted her. His gaze snagged on her movements with the blue towel—a blue that matched the cornflower of her eyes—as she dabbed it delicately against the sides of her heart-shaped face, her dripping hair. He ached to take the towel from her. Perform the task himself. He fought the urge. "Are you saying you don't love your husband?"

The question made her laugh. "I despise him."

"You do?" Why had he said that? He should have said, *I see*. No one was more aware than he was of that fine line between love and hate. He could not take her declaration at face value. It might not mean she actually despised her husband.

David took a swallow of wine. It wasn't necessarily that she'd come here because she felt something for him, either. She might just be lashing out—a normal response from someone betrayed by a lover. "Then— forgive my rudeness—why are you so upset?"

"I—I..."

"I won't judge you, Eden. Surely you know me well enough by now to know that." She looked like a startled deer about to bolt. David respected her instincts. He should let her leave. Dear God, he *had* to let her leave. "I'm a good listener."

"Yes, I know." He was a wonderful listener. A sliver of guilt stabbed Eden. If only counsel were all that she longed for from David. "I didn't know where else to turn. But I've changed my mind."

She took a gulp of wine, then spun away from him, set her glass on the hearth and lifted one foot toward a wet shoe. "Coming here was not a good idea."

"Why?" David swore under his breath. What had he been thinking? Doing? She'd arrived undeniably upset, and here he was plying her with alcohol and fighting his desire for her—which he was obviously doing a lousy job of hiding.

"Because what I want from you is too much to ask." Eden's shoe was too damp. Her bare foot stuck on the wet leather. She jerked her hand to her mouth, but not before a small cry slipped out and into the room like the helpless wail of a wounded animal.

"Oh, Eden." David's will shattered into a thousand pieces at the neediness in the small sob. He closed the gap between them, set his glass on the hearth, grasped her by the shoulders and pulled her around. "Good Lord, you're soaked."

"It's raining," she said lamely. Her wide blue eyes were awash with tears.

"You should get out of those clothes . . . let me . . ." His voice choked with desire. "Let me throw them in the dryer."

"No. I'll be fine." Her gaze stole to the dab of shaving cream still nestling his earlobe, and without thinking, she snagged a corner of the towel at his neck and blotted it away.

David groaned in sweet agony. He hadn't been with a woman since . . . since he'd met Eden. Surely, after all these months of celibacy, he could find the strength to suppress the need that was tearing through his veins, burning his restraint as efficiently as the fire was burning the logs. He yanked the towel from around his neck, tossed it aside and struggled to keep his voice level. "Eden, I—"

"Oh, David." The desire in his soft green eyes plucked at the unplayed strings of her heart and filled her soul with a mesmerizing melody, promising love and untold joys. "Is it so wrong of me to need you, David, as protector, confidant, friend? To want you as I want you now, in every way a woman wants a man?"

He caught her hand and kissed her palm. The contact sent a frisson up her arm and straight into her heart. She ought to pull away, resist. "Tell me it's not my imagination. You do feel something for me, don't you?"

David couldn't believe he had heard correctly. He tried speaking but could only nod. Had Eden just admitted that she had tender feelings for him? He wanted to shout his love for her, but she stiffened suddenly. He hesitated.

A look of distress captured her features. "I can't do this. I'm putting you on the spot, ethically and professionally and personally. You deserve better from me."

"Let me be the judge of that." His voice rasped over the words, the loneliness in his soul reaching out to her.

Eden blinked, tried forcing down the lump in her throat, tried catching her breath. But all of it was impossible...with him standing so close, his hands infusing her damp shoulders with heat, his ragged breath caressing her face, his head lowering.

She raised her face to his and closed her eyes as David's mouth claimed hers, sweeping her into a whirlwind of passion that seemed to go on and on, stealing her senses and wrapping her in a velvet cocoon.

She was not conscious of peeling off her wet clothes, only of standing naked before David, brazenly, as she had never done with another man. The awe in his eyes thrilled her, humbled her, sent her passion spiraling higher and higher, and she welcomed his hesitant touches as he gently buffed her damp skin with the fluffy blue towel.

Then he was kissing her again, on her mouth, on her face, on her neck. "Oh, David, I've longed for this, longed for you," she murmured, holding his head in both hands, her fingers luxuriating in the velvety texture of his thick brown hair. He lifted his head; the mossy green of his eyes had darkened to jade with his desire for her.

He murmured, "I can't believe this is happening. That you're really here. Like this."

Her heart drummed in rhythm to the rain striking the windows, a beat that was savage and wild and beautiful.

"Neither can I." It was a million dreams come true. Eden shoved the terry robe down David's back, her fingertips playing over the muscled flesh of his broad shoulders and defined arms, across the crisp brown hair of his wide chest, and she savored each delicious new sensation.

With a honeyed groan, David lifted her against his chest, bringing his naked need against her own, pulling a breathless gasp from her and lowering her to the floor beneath him, gazing at her with such want in his eyes she knew that until this moment she had never understood what it meant to be a woman.

She welcomed his passionate invasion of her most intimate stronghold, reveled in the taut, silken friction of his sensual thrusts, meeting his rhythm with equal fervor, their joining like a match struck against slate, the explosion fast and hard, rocketing through her every vein, every nerve, every limb, aftershocks tingling her toes and fingertips, the soles of her feet, the roots of her hair.

Never in her twenty-eight years had she experienced anything close to this mind-boggling pleasure, this achingly sweet joy. "I didn't know making love could feel so...good."

David gave her a lopsided grin, then lifted her hand and kissed her fingers. "I dreamed it could."

"Did you, David?" Eden trailed her fingertips tentatively over his chest and gazed into his moss green eyes.

"Night and day."

Her heart gave a happy leap. If he'd thought about it night and day, it meant he'd wanted to be with her as much as she had wanted to be with him. Everything seemed suddenly less bleak. She felt as if she'd come home, home to the one man who would always make her feel safe and . . . loved.

Loved? She realized with a jolt that she was fooling herself. She was neither safe nor loved. What David had said was dear, but he'd made no real declarations. No promises. Why should he? Dismayed, Eden shoved herself to a sitting position, grabbed up the blue towel and wrapped it around herself like a toga, closing her eyes against the anxious knot that once again filled her stomach. The fire seemed suddenly too hot against her backside.

"What have I done? I'm no better than Peter." And when David learned the whole story, he'd feel as if she'd just used him.

"Don't say that. You never cheated on Peter while the marriage was intact. He's set you free." David touched her shoulder. Eden flinched as if he'd burned her. *What had he done to her?* Shaking his head, he grabbed his robe and scooted onto the couch. The thought of the misery he was causing her ate a hole through the afterglow he'd been feeling.

He'd compromised her, compromised his ethics. . . . Why in hell had he acted so rashly, been so quick to believe that Eden might love him as much as he loved her?

He clenched his hands in his lap to keep from reaching out to her again. "I'm the one who let things get out of hand."

"No. I wanted this as much as you did." Afraid her feelings would be crushed, afraid David didn't love her as she loved him, Eden borrowed a phrase she'd read in a women's magazine. "Please, can we just let it be what it was—a wonderful reaffirmation of life?"

"Sure." His heart dropped like a deflated balloon. Was that all it had meant to her? A validation of her desirability? It had meant so very much more to him.

Eden read the confusion and hurt on David's face and wondered if she'd misjudged the depth of his feeling for her. But what would he feel when he heard the whole truth? She had held it in long enough. She lurched to her feet, awkward in the mammoth towel. "I haven't told you the worst."

Frowning, David shrugged on his robe.

Her confidence faltered. She drew a bracing breath and blurted, "Peter is dropping Beth from his insurance."

Concern grabbed his handsome face. He was acutely aware of Beth's dire condition, her long wait for a kidney donor. "But that would knock her down the waiting list. Maybe off of it completely. Doesn't he know that?"

"Of course he does. He doesn't care. As far as Peter is concerned, Beth is the main reason for our marriage falling apart."

"Her illness, you mean?"

"Yes."

"That's quite common. I deal every week with families struggling to stay together after a serious illness or injury has befallen one of them."

Eden gave a bitter laugh. "Peter resents the time demands she places on me."

David knew he was too close to this to be impartial; he'd abandoned his objectivity the moment he'd touched her. But he could understand how a husband would resent a lack of attention from his wife, especially a wife like Eden, especially a man like Peter Prescott, whom David suspected was a selfish bastard. "Beth didn't wish the disease on herself."

"Exactly." Eden was gripping the towel with white knuckles. "But I can't let him take away her insurance. It's a death sentence for her. What am I going to do?"

So help him God, he wanted to fold her into his arms again. He clenched his fists. "Have you seen a lawyer yet?"

She shook her head. "I'm not sure it will do me any good."

"Why? This is a community-property state. A clever attorney might be able to finagle a settlement that keeps Beth's insurance coverage in lieu of other concessions to Peter."

He didn't doubt for a moment that Eden would agree to such a settlement—even if it meant a substantial financial loss for her—with Beth's life at stake. So why had she paled at the suggestion?

She didn't keep him in the dark. "I signed a prenuptial agreement."

Of course. He should have realized. A man of Prescott's wealth would insist on a prenuptial agreement. "I take it the document doesn't serve your best interests."

A terse laugh burst from her, and she grimaced. "Not unless Peter conveniently dies before the divorce is final."

"What?"

Eden brought her hand to her mouth, realizing belatedly how heartless she sounded. "I didn't mean that. I'm not wishing Peter dead." Nor was she explaining this coherently. She took another breath. "The terms of the agreement state that if he dies before me, the estate will be divided between his sister and me. But if we divorce, I'll get nothing." She began to tremble. "Without the insurance, Beth will die."

"No. You won't allow that." And neither would he. There were a few sources he would investigate first thing tomorrow. But until he had, he wouldn't mention them, wouldn't give her false hope. But he could offer real hope. "Eden, there has to be something you can do. Talk to an attorney about it. I know you'll find a way."

"Find a way?" Desperation nipped at her. Since she'd learned last year that Beth's kidneys were failing and that she was not a possible donor, Eden had dedicated every waking hour to her sister's welfare. It had been a horror watching the lively twenty-two-year-old college student transform into a walking ghost, so tired most days she did little more than sleep. Damn Peter Prescott's cold heart. If she didn't stop him from going through with the divorce, Beth would die. "The only 'way' I'll find is to stop Peter."

She gathered her clothes and rushed down the hall to the bathroom. Minutes later she was dressed, damp fabric sticking to her warmed flesh, chilling her again. But her mind was so full, she ignored the physical discomfort. She wanted to avoid David, to leave without trying to deal with the further complication in her life that their lovemaking had created.

But he was waiting outside the bathroom door. He had donned jeans and a T-shirt. "Eden, please don't leave like this."

"I have to." She brushed past him.

He followed her to the foyer. "Let me help. I'll do *anything* it takes. Stay and talk about it."

"Not now. I just can't...." Still, she appreciated his offer. She paused at the open door, rose up on tiptoe and kissed him lightly on the lips. "I'll call you later."

"I'll hold you to that." David hated letting her go. "You need to change into dry clothes. Promise me you'll go straight home."

"I promise."

But for the next few hours, Eden drove aimlessly through the rain-washed streets of Seattle, crossed the 520 floating bridge into Bellevue, then drove down 405 to I-90 and back into Seattle, repeating the route several times, hardly noticing either the cities' night lights or the demands of the heavy traffic.

Her mind puzzled over the dilemmas of Peter and the insurance, of David and the wonderful way he'd made her feel, the awful way she'd left things between them. In her mind's eye, she recalled his glorious naked body, remembered how brazen she'd been in their lovemaking, how abandoned. Heat stole through her.

With Peter she always held something back, never even permitted the lights on. She had been his possession, his showpiece, the prettiest wife in a room full of pretty wives, something to make other men envious of him—a role she detested.

A role that ended when Beth's illness began taking its toll on her energy. Her looks.

Then Peter had made certain she knew just how undesirable she'd become, demanding his marital rights but twice in the past year. She shuddered as she thought of the last time, only two weeks ago. Peter had been drunk and in a vicious mood. She'd gritted her teeth until he'd finished.

But with David everything had been so different. Did he love her? Just a little? The delicious warmth rushed through her again. He hadn't seemed to notice the circles under her eyes, the weight she'd lost. He'd made her feel special, alluring, and in turn she'd trusted him with her every vulnerability, knowing he'd neither ridicule nor scorn her.

Eden stretched. If she trusted David to this degree, shouldn't she trust his advice? Maybe there was some other way to cover the cost of Beth's transplant surgery and recovery. Making up her mind to call an attorney first thing in the morning, she left the freeway behind and headed for the Issaquah Plateau.

A mile from home, she stopped for gas. It was nearly 2:00 a.m. when she arrived home and pulled into the five-car garage. Peter's Porsche was still gone. He hadn't told her to move out yet, but he would soon enough. Well, she'd deal with that when the time came.

She entered the kitchen. The phone was ringing. Fearing it might awaken Beth or Ariel Bell, her nurse, both of whom slept on this floor, or Peter's sister, Valerie, who slept in the room directly above the kitchen, she grabbed the receiver. "Hello."

An unfamiliar voice said, "Mrs. Peter Prescott, please."

"Speaking."

"Mrs. Prescott, this is Detective Kollecki with the Issaquah Police Department. I'd like to come over and speak with you."

"Now?" At this hour? Eden's heartbeat accelerated. "What about?"

"About your husband."

Eden gripped the phone tighter. "H-has Peter been in an accident?" He always drove his car too fast.

"I'd rather not say over the phone."

An odd queasiness washed over Eden. It had been a horrendous day. Apparently it wasn't over. Then again, was this really the police? She insisted on phoning the caller back to verify his identity. A moment later, after looking up the phone number, she had the Issaquah police on the line and was put through to Detective Kollecki, who still insisted on telling her about Peter in person. Her queasiness worsened. "You'd better come right over."

They arrived fifteen minutes later. Two of them, dressed in plainclothes. Kollecki was a stockily built man with bright red hair and Santa cheeks. Eden didn't catch the other officer's name. "Please, just tell me what's happened to Peter."

"I'm sorry, ma'am, but we found your husband earlier this evening. He's dead." Kollecki grimaced. "It looks like murder."

Chapter Two

"M-murder?" Eden stared at Kollecki with disbelieving eyes, but the shock of his words was sinking in, stepping up her already thudding heartbeat. "How—how could that be?"

Kollecki seemed to be reading her reactions, measuring her responses as if she was taking an oral test he would later grade. "There's no question about it, ma'am. The medical examiner was definite."

Definite. Peter was dead. *Murdered.* Her hand flew to her mouth. It was unbelievable. She noticed Kollecki's intense dark eyes sweeping her, taking in every detail of her, from her rumpled clothing to the mascara she knew was smudged beneath her eyes. But whatever he deduced from this she could not guess.

"May we come in, ma'am? There are a few questions we'd like to ask."

Eden led them into the formal living room, switching on lamps before perching on the edge of the sofa. Her mind reeled, her body felt hot and cold at the same time and the glare from the table lamps seemed as harshly bright as if their shades were missing.

Kollecki sat across from her, dwarfing the delicate Queen Anne chair, his dun-colored raincoat dull against the gold-striped brocade cushions. He glanced at a tablet nestled in his thick hand. "Do you know a... Shannon Smalley?"

The question startled her. A rush of heat beat a path up her spine and into her face. Did she know Peter's new love? Oh, yes. Only too well. But why was he asking her this? Her brows tugged together. "Ms. Smalley is Dr. Dayton, er, our dentist's receptionist."

"Do you know where she lives?"

Eden stiffened. "Why?"

"Then you don't?"

"Really, Officer Kollecki, I don't how you found out about Peter's—" Eden stopped herself.

But it was all Kollecki needed to hear. "So you knew about them. For how long?"

A huge sigh pushed through her lips. "About eight hours...I suppose."

"I see." He jotted something on the tablet.

The emotional tide she'd staved off during the past several hours threatened to overwhelm her. Tears stung her eyes. She struggled against them; she would not cry in front of these men. She cleared her throat and somehow kept her voice level. "Look, I'll cooperate fully, but it's nearly 3:00 a.m. It's been a hell of a day and it isn't over yet. Could your questions wait until morning?"

The two men exchanged a secret glance, then Kollecki folded his tablet into his pocket. "Sure. Call me around ten."

Moments later the two policemen were back in their car. Kollecki gazed out at the huge house as his partner started the engine. "What did you make of her?"

"Cool. Like ice." His partner smirked. "Her old man's offed and she don't even ask how."

Kollecki nodded. "Or where."

PATCHES OF BLUE in the cloudy sky gave David hope that the day would be a good one—even though he was off to a late start. He'd tossed and turned throughout the long night, dreaming of Eden, of making love to her, worrying about her state of mind. All he wanted to do was call her, just hear her voice, just talk to her. She'd promised to call. Why hadn't she? He'd give her until noon. If he hadn't heard by then, he'd drive to her house.

He hauled his briefcase to his side, pulled open his front door and stepped onto the porch. He felt something under his right foot. Glancing down, he saw he'd crushed a flower. The moisture left his mouth, and a chill like icy water sluiced down his spine. It was a rose.

A single white rose.

Was this someone's idea of a sick joke? Staggering back, he jerked his head up. The only people around were his neighbors going about their morning routines. He drew a shaky breath, then squatted and examined the flower. It had stopped raining sometime near midnight. The rose was dry.

Should he call the police? And...what? Ask if any of his friends or students were missing? Had been found dead? His pulse raced, and David willed himself to calm down. He was being paranoid. Unnerved for no reason.

Besides, whom would he call about it? That unpleasant detective who'd handled Marianne DePaul's case? He gave a bitter laugh. He sure as hell didn't want to open *that* can of worms.

Not without just cause.

He hurried back inside and brought out a Ziploc bag, then, using a pencil, he lifted the crushed flower and deposited it within. Kollecki. That was the police officer's name, David recalled with accompanying distaste. The cop had actually suspected him of killing Marianne. If Rose Hatcher hadn't confessed . . .

It didn't bear thinking about. Yet on the drive to work, old fears and guilts pecked at him. Was the rose significant in another crime? Or had it been placed on his porch as a symbol of love? Maybe by Eden? No. It had still been raining when Eden left. She wouldn't have returned.

However, just thinking about Eden eased the tension gripping him. He hummed along with a CD the rest of the way to the University of Washington Medical Center. He occupied a two-room office on the sixteenth floor of the BB Tower, a seventeen-story structure attached to the east side of the hospital.

He hurried through the busy halls, certain Colleen MacLaine, his secretary of the past year, had beaten him in, a rare occurrence. The aroma of fresh coffee greeted him, confirming his assumption as he entered the main door and giving him the first sense of normalcy he'd had since last night.

Colleen looked up from her desk, her large, cobalt blue eyes lighting at the sight of him. "Get held up in traffic?"

"Slept through the alarm." It was a wonder he'd slept at all.

"You probably needed the extra rest." Colleen's fawn brown hair was twined in a French braid with a forest green ribbon at its tip that matched the color of her severely cut suit. Her face was pretty, her manner demure, emphasized by the crisp white blouse she wore buttoned to her chin.

He set his briefcase, with the Ziploc bag tucked inside, on the floor beside Colleen's desk, strode to the coffeemaker and snatched up his regular cup. He never should have allowed Eden to run out last night. Who knew what was going on in that beautiful head of hers this morning? Maybe he should call her now.

He noticed Colleen was grimacing as she did when she had something to tell him she knew he wouldn't like. "What?"

"Uh, Ms. Prescott arrived about ten minutes ago. She insisted on waiting in your office."

It was his strict policy that no one wait unattended in his private office. David pulled his mouth into a flat line, and in justification of herself, Colleen added, "She was so very upset."

He nodded. "It's all right."

Colleen's shoulders sagged in relief. "I gave her some coffee."

"Good." Anxious to see Eden, he finished filling his own cup, then swung open his office door, speaking her name before he saw her. "Eden?"

But it wasn't Eden waiting in the high-backed chair across from his desk. Peter Prescott's sister, Valerie, rose to her full five feet nine inches and whirled around to face him. One vivid ginger eyebrow arched like an arrow toward her slicked-back auburn hair. "Eden? Surely you aren't expecting her *this* morning?"

David flinched. No, he supposed he wasn't expecting Eden *this* morning. Drawing in the scent of Valerie's perfume—an aroma that brought to mind again the white rose on his doorstep—David wondered anew who'd left it and why.

His office, as all the windowed offices on this floor, had three glass panels, separated by chrome frames, set high in the end wall above a chest-high heating system that ran the length of the wall. Only the middle window could be opened, and that could only be opened with a special key kept by security.

Besides his desk and two high-backed leather chairs, his own contributions to the decor, there were built-in bookshelves, two shoulder-height metal filing cabinets and an easy chair in the corner. Colleen had contributed two jade plants that reposed atop the heating unit and thrived with her care.

Distracted, David skirted his desk and set his cup on its satiny walnut finish, and it occurred to him that he had not expected Valerie this morning, either. She was no longer his patient, hadn't been since about a month or more before she'd recommended Eden and Beth to him.

But Colleen was right; something had Valerie terribly upset. Her hazel eyes were red-streaked and puffy as if from crying. Usually only her beloved brother, Peter, reduced her to tears. He couldn't help wondering if Prescott had burned Valerie with that acid tongue of his in the wake of asking Eden for a divorce. "Did we have an appointment, Valerie?"

"No. But—" She choked on a sob. Tears sprang to her eyes and spilled down her cheeks. "I—I thought you'd understand."

David instantly regretted the brusque tone in his voice. Surely he could spare her a few minutes. "Understand what?"

"That I'd need to talk to you. H-how am I going to go on . . . now that he's been killed?"

David's confusion deepened. His mind was too crammed with his own worries to decipher what Valerie was saying. He schooled his patience and said gently, "Perhaps you should start from the beginning. Who's been killed?"

"Why, Peter, of course. Haven't you listened to a radio? Read a newspaper? He was murdered last night by that—that ungrateful wife of his."

"What?" David's mouth dropped onto his chest and hung open like a sprung door. "How?"

Valerie withdrew a lace hankie from the sleeve of her black dress and waved it at him, wafting her rosy scent across the expanse of the desk, before she brought it to her nose and sniffled. "Shot him...probably with my little gun...it's missing, you know. And that rude policeman said Peter was killed with a small-caliber weapon."

David felt as if a bullet had pierced his own heart. Eden? Never. She wasn't capable of murder. He gripped the arms of his chair. But he dare not contradict Valerie. Their years of therapy had unmasked her jealousy of Eden, a resentment that had started the moment Peter proposed marriage.

Dear God, when had Prescott been killed? Where? At home? A sheet of ice spread through his belly, and he couldn't bring himself to ask. Had the police arrested Eden? "Wh-where is Eden now?"

Valerie sat straighter, obviously affronted by the concern in his voice. "Home, with Beth. Hasn't even shed a single tear. But dear Beth hasn't taken the news much better than I. She's so fragile, you know. Like me, I suppose." She cleared her throat, and fresh tears trickled down her cheeks. "Could you possibly give me some more of those little mood pills? I can't seem to quit shaking or crying.''

If Peter had been murdered at the home, the police would surely have declared it a crime scene and required the women to move out during the investigation. He breathed slightly easier.

"Dr. Coulter?" Valerie snuffled.

David gave her a sympathetic smile. "I'm sorry, Valerie. Sorry about your loss and that I can't help you with a prescription. You're no longer my patient. I suggest you see your M.D."

LYNZY ANDERS, David's student assistant, was conferring with Colleen over the morning newspaper when he came out of his office minutes after Valerie left. Colleen turned back to her typewriter.

But his student assistant made no pretense of working. She shoved her shoulder-length, straight, dark brown hair away from her oval face. The young woman's appearance was all what-you-see-is-what-you-get. But something in the depths of her coffee brown eyes had long made him wonder at the sensitivity hidden behind her normally friendly-clown attitude. She poked the newspaper. "Have you seen this?"

Still reeling from the news, he moved closer and peered over her shoulder at the front page of the *Seattle Times*. Peter Prescott's photo stood out beneath the headline Local Businessman Murdered. "No. But it seems I'm the only one in town who hasn't."

"Not Prescott," Lynzy said, annoyed impatience in her tone. "The woman who was killed with him."

Valerie hadn't mentioned any woman being killed with Prescott. His gut clenched. Peter's new lady?

Lynzy tapped the article, arching her neck to look back and up at him. "Shannon Smalley."

"Shannon was with Peter Prescott?" Stunned disbelief jackknifed his knees, and David dropped onto the chair beside his secretary's desk. Shannon was supposed to have had dinner with him last night, but she'd called to say she was spending the night with...Pete. Peter Prescott? Shannon was the woman Prescott had left Eden for? He muttered, "Not Shannon and Peter Prescott?"

"Yes." Lynzy nodded with macabre relish. "They were murdered at her house in Klahanie—one of those housing developments in the Issaquah Plateau."

Colleen stopped typing and twisted in her swivel chair. Her eyes seemed as round as cue balls. "I don't understand what a rich guy who rubbed elbows with the movers and shakers of the world was even doing with someone like *her.*"

"Come on, girl." Lynzy rolled her eyes. "It's so obvious. Read between the lines."

The secretary blushed crimson. "But how would he even know her? She was a dental receptionist."

"*My* dentist's receptionist," David answered in a flat voice, adding almost to himself, "I think the Prescotts are also Dr. Dayton's patients...probably where Prescott met her."

He scanned the article, seeking details, needing explanations for the unexplainable. The words seemed to blur. Shock waves rocked David, pitching him back in time, dredging up his own connection to Shannon...and her older sister—a friend of Colleen's, who also happened to be a nurse in the transplant wing of this very hospital.

Lynzy scooted one miniskirted hip onto Colleen's desk, revealing the edge of a small rose tattoo just above her knee. Swinging a long, boot-clad leg to some beat of her own, she said, "You do remember . . . her name was on Rose Hatcher's hit list."

He hadn't forgotten. He doubted Lynzy or Colleen had forgotten, either.

Colleen fingered her high collar as if it were choking her. "Your name and mine were also on that list, Lynzy."

"Yeah, it gives me goose bumps just remembering. Hey, Doc, you haven't gotten any more white roses, have you?"

David felt the heat drain from his face.

"I was just kidding, Doc." Lynzy's nervous laugh died. "Hey, are you all right? You're kind of green."

But David didn't hear her; his mind was on the crushed rose. What did it mean? Why had it been left on his doorstep? Was someone trying to make him think Shannon was dead because of him? All he'd done was recommend her for the receptionist's job. David rubbed his eyes with the flat of his hand. No. *This* time had nothing to do with *that* time. Rose Hatcher was locked away. She couldn't have killed Shannon.

But someone had. Eden's words rang through his head. *The only way is to stop Peter.* No! His stomach roiled. He clenched his fists.

Lynzy touched his arm. "Doc, maybe you should lie down in your office for a while."

David shook his head. "No. I—I have an errand to run."

Afraid and shell-shocked, torn between rushing to Eden and taking the rose to the police, he snatched up his briefcase, which he'd forgotten beside Colleen's desk. "Reschedule this morning's appointments. I can be reached on my car phone if the need arises."

He darted out into a day that now promised to be anything but a good one, and five minutes later telephoned Eden's house. Her recorded voice asked him to leave a message after the beep. Frustrated, he punched the Off button and dropped the phone on the seat beside his briefcase, which contained the crushed rose. Eden could be screening calls, but he wasn't about to leave a message that anyone might overhear.

Say, Valerie. Or the police.

The heavy freeway traffic tried his patience, and by the time he reached Issaquah, his nerves were frayed. Front Street traffic was even worse: stop-and-go. The half-mile drive to Sunset Way took ten minutes. He drew a ragged breath as he finally pulled into a parking space at the Issaquah police station. Staring at the building, he felt as if the whole awful nightmare had started again. Or that it had never ended.

AT THE ISSAQUAH police station, Eden sat in a windowless room that smelled of stale cigarette smoke and depression. The overhead light was glaringly bright, and the headache she'd had all night had worsened into a steady, thumping pain, like a sledgehammer slamming against her temples.

With her back to the open door, she waited on an uncomfortable chair, her shaking hands clenched in her lap as she tried blocking out the memory of how Peter had looked when she'd gone to identify his body an hour earlier. How could someone be so alive one moment and so...so—? She jammed her hand against her belly. There was no associating the vital man she'd lived with for seven years with that cold object lying on a slab in the King County Morgue.

Voices filtered in from an open door down the hallway, bits and pieces of conversation. Desperate for a distraction, she listened. "Shannon Smalley...why do I...connect her with...shrink Coulter?"

Eden's spine stiffened. Were they talking about David? She craned to hear better.

"Her name...the hit list that deranged student of the doc's who murdered—"

Eden lost the last few words, but then the louder of the two voices boomed clearly. "Hah! I remember now. Man, I don't like coincidences."

A door banged shut, cutting off the rest of the conversation. The stagnant air in the small room seemed thicker than ever, and Eden felt as if her lungs couldn't draw in enough oxygen to keep her alive. Of course, David knew Shannon Smalley from Dr. Dayton's office, but if she'd understood correctly, Shannon had somehow been involved in the death of that student of his a while back. But how?

Footsteps behind her sent the thought scurrying. Every nerve in her body felt pinched as Kollecki entered and kicked the door shut. His dark red hair was slicked off his high forehead as if he'd just showered and hadn't bothered to dry it. He carried two disposable cups of steaming liquid. "Thought you'd like some coffee."

"Thank you." The words came out raspy. Her mouth was too dry, but the taste of bile at the back of her throat kept her from reaching for the coffee cup he set near her hand.

He scraped back a chair and sat opposite her, pulled a tablet and pen from his suit pocket, flipped through a few pages, then lifted his dark, intense gaze to her. "Now, Mrs. Prescott, what time did you last see your husband?"

"Yesterday, around 6:00 p.m." She focused on *that* image of Peter, shoving the other vile one away, shoving the worrisome thoughts of David further yet.

"Would that be the same time he told you about his affair with Miss Smalley?"

As if reaching for a lifeline, Eden curled her small, trembling hands around the cup. Last night she'd wished for someone to discuss her problems with, but never in her wildest imaginings had she envisioned it would be a police detective. But it was, and under the circumstances, she decided, honesty was probably the best policy. "My husband wasn't just having an affair with Ms. Smalley, he intended to marry her."

Kollecki's eyebrows twitched. "So he wanted a divorce?"

Eden nodded, suspecting he already knew that.

"Did you argue the point?"

"No." She shook her head. "No one argued with Peter."

"So a divorce was okay with you?"

Eden took a gulp of coffee. Hot and acrid, it rolled over her tongue and landed in her queasy stomach like a fiery ball of oil. Yesterday at this time, the answer to that question would likely have been a resounding no.

But by the time she'd arrived home last night, determined to find a lawyer who'd stave off Peter's intention of dropping Beth from his insurance, she could honestly say she'd come to terms with the idea.

Of course, a good deal of the credit was David's. He'd helped her rediscover her self-respect and shown her that there were marvelous experiences awaiting her in this life. She stared at the dark coffee. "I wasn't sorry the marriage was over, if that's what you're asking."

"Oh, really?" Kollecki studied her, then checked his notepad. "According to your sister-in-law, you signed an ironclad prenuptial agreement."

Eden glanced at the wall behind him. What could she say? There was no justifying being young and naive, being just plain stupid, being so desperate for a better life she'd jumped at the first offer. "Yes, I did."

"Ms. Prescott says you inherit half of your deceased husband's estate now."

Ice threaded her heart. "That's a term of the agreement."

"How fortunate for you that he was killed before he could get his divorce."

She gasped, jerking her gaze back to Kollecki's. "What a vicious thing to say! Lots of people have lousy marriages, Peter and I included. But I never wished him dead."

She glared at him but could no longer keep at bay the awful image from the morgue. The coffee churned in her stomach. She was going to be sick. "I couldn't kill anyone."

"Your sister-in-law seems to have a different opinion."

"She's high-strung. She became hysterical at the news and accused everyone whose name popped into her head, including poor Beth." Eden had paid little attention. Surely the police weren't giving Valerie's ravings credence? Fear crawled through her. "Valerie was very attached to her brother."

"I heard he didn't treat her well."

Eden's eyebrows shot up. Who would have told him a thing like that? Not Valerie, not Beth and not her.

Beth's nurse? Ariel Bell might have overheard conversations and related tales of, or perhaps been the victim of, Peter's sharp tongue. It would certainly explain Ariel's dislike of him.

"I need to know where you were last night between nine and midnight."

Eden shoved the coffee to one side. The ache inside her head vied with the pain in her stomach. She'd left David's around nine. She massaged her temples with her fingertips. If only she'd gone directly home, then Beth or her nurse might still have been awake and could have verified her whereabouts. Then perhaps telling Kollecki she'd been at David's would help. But now...

If the police discovered she was in love with David, had made love to David... Shivers raced over her flesh as she recalled the things she'd said to David, realizing how they must sound to him now, how her words could be used against her. Motive. She had it in spades.

And what about David and his declaration that he'd do *anything* he could to help her? What about his connection to Shannon Smalley? The fear inside her leapt another three notches. She decided not to mention David—unless it became absolutely necessary. "I...just drove around... for hours."

"Can anyone verify that?"

The only thing anyone could verify was that she'd stopped for gas sometime around 2:00 a.m. "I was alone."

"Too bad."

There was no mistaking the threat in his gently spoken words. Eden's pulse stepped up a beat.

"After Peter's declaration...I needed to think." Even though she spoke the truth, she heard how desperate and lame it sounded. There was an odd, tinny taste on her tongue.

Kollecki referred to his notebook, flipped a page, then another. Slowly his gaze lifted. "I'll ask you the same question I asked last night. Do you know where Shannon Smalley lived?"

"Yes." Last night she hadn't known the significance of this question. Now she did. Bile climbed her throat. She swallowed hard. "Do I need a lawyer?"

His eyebrows twitched almost imperceptibly. "That's up to you."

Eden felt like a cornered mouse about to be eaten by the sly cat. Her fear escalated to terror. Somehow she managed to sound calmer than she'd thought possible. "I think I'd better call my attorney."

"All right." He stood and gathered his tablet and pen.

"Am—am I free to go?"

The look in Kollecki's dark eyes chilled Eden almost as much as his words. "For now."

Chapter Three

As David locked his car, he glanced around the parking lot; just behind Front Street, it was shaped like a long salmon and accommodated the police station, the library, a small park and several businesses. There was an erratic flow of automobile and foot traffic.

A petite woman hurrying from the police station grabbed his attention. *Eden.* He caught up with her as she reached her minivan. "Eden, I just heard."

She spun around, blinking at him. "David?"

"I—" Her appearance eclipsed the rest of his thought; she looked as if she were on the verge of collapse. Dark circles underscored her eyes, a sure sign that she'd slept little, if at all. He longed to pull her into his arms but resisted. This parking lot was too public and too close to the very department investigating her husband's murder.

"Why are you here?" She took a step closer to him. "Not to see Kollecki?" So Kollecki was in charge of this case, too. His stomach clenched. "I, ah, yes, I am."

Apprehension leapt into her eyes. "I didn't tell him I was with you last night. I was hoping you wouldn't mention it, either—at least until we could talk."

"I'm not seeing Kollecki about you." David's grip on his briefcase had his knuckles aching and his imagination working overtime, conjuring visions of the briefcase being transparent, the rose exposed to view. "It's another matter altogether."

God, he prayed that was the truth.

Eden's eyes narrowed, and a frown furrowed her smooth forehead. "Shannon Smalley?"

The moisture left his mouth. "How did you know?"

She seemed about to say something, but a patrol car arrived and stole her attention. Apprehension reappeared in her eyes, and when she spoke, it was almost a whisper. "Not here."

"Where, when?" David lowered his own voice. "Name it."

Yet again her attention was diverted by a car pulling into a reserved police space. David glanced over his shoulder. The man who sat behind the wheel was staring at them. There was something familiar about him. "Who's that?"

"The detective who came to the house last night with Kollecki," Eden whispered, then raised her voice loudly enough for anyone within earshot to hear. "Thank you for your condolences, Dr. Coulter. Beth is expecting me for lunch."

With that, she wheeled around and climbed into her van.

He wanted to snatch her back, to kiss away her pain, her apprehension. Instead, feeling the same cold panic he'd felt at finding the rose, David stepped away from the van. The engine roared to life. He fell into step four paces behind the detective who'd been staring at Eden and him, recalling now that he'd been the other investigator on Marianne DePaul's case.

Detective Ron Tagg. That was his name. He was me-
dium height with a reed-thin body, gray hair and, as
David remembered, a reasonable disposition. Maybe he
could talk to Tagg about the rose instead of Kollecki.

But Kollecki insisted on being included. The three
men sat around the oblong table in the windowless interrogation room. The rose, in its Ziploc bag, reposed
on the table. Kollecki wrote David a receipt for it, then,
handing it to him, leveled his cold, dark eyes at him.

David hated the crawling feeling dealing with Kollecki gave him. "So, what do you think?"

Kollecki's gaze grew measured. "It may or may not
be a piece of the puzzle."

"I thought it might be someone's idea of a sick joke."
David tugged on his ear. The truth was, a part of him
still clung to that idea. He wanted it to be a disgusting
coincidence, wanted Kollecki and Tagg to confirm it.

"Could be we've got us a copycat killer." Tagg had
the gravelly voice of a heavy smoker.

"Copycat?" A sinking feeling dragged the bottom
from David's stomach. "You mean that Shannon, not
Prescott, could have been the main target?"

Tagg shrugged. "Could be someone just wants us to
think copycat."

"Could be someone closer to home killed these people." Kollecki puffed out his Santa cheeks. "How well
did you know Shannon Smalley?"

"Pretty well—as I told you last winter." David
squirmed uncomfortably on the straight-backed seat.
Had Kollecki just questioned Eden in this drab room?
"Shannon is...was the kid sister of a nurse who works
in the U-Dub's transplant wing. Denise Smalley is a
friend of my secretary's. That's how I came to recom-

mend her for the job with Dr. Dayton, and subsequently Shannon and I became friends.''

Kollecki glanced at his tablet, then lifted his shrewd gaze. ''My sources say you were more than friends. Any truth to that?''

''None.'' What sources? Disquiet twined David's heart. ''We were *only* friends. We had dinner together occasionally, but it was strictly platonic. In fact, I was supposed to dine with her last night, but she canceled at the last minute to be with Pete. I had no idea 'Pete' was Peter Prescott.''

''You knew Prescott?''

''No. His sister is my former patient, and his sister-in-law is presently a patient, but I'd never met the man.''

''But you do know the beautiful widow.''

It was not a question, and David disliked the implications. ''You make it sound like I have a harem of women, Detective. I don't. I do know a lot of women. Most of them professionally. But I seldom date. As to Mrs. Prescott—I just told you, her sister, Beth, is my patient.''

Kollecki lifted a hand in an innocent gesture. ''Hey, I didn't mean to push any buttons, Doctor.''

Like hell he didn't.

David guessed Kollecki had heard about Eden and him talking in the parking lot. Kollecki might not yet know how intimately Eden and he knew one another, but David feared it was only a matter of time before he found out.

''If that's all—'' David tucked the receipt for the rose into his suit pocket and stood ''—I have patients to see this afternoon.''

"Of course." Kollecki shoved up and out of his own chair. "And let's not mention the rose to anyone else for now."

"All right," David agreed.

"But if any more of these show up—" Tagg grasped the Ziploc bag and shook it at him "—or if you recall anything else . . ."

"I'll let you know immediately."

Kollecki let him out the locked door that led to the parking lot. David wanted to go straight to Eden and figure out what was going on. But as he started toward the parking area, he encountered Denise Smalley standing outside the double glass doors that accessed the waiting room; she was leaning against the brick wall, smoking.

Her hair, a mix of bleached and natural ash blond, was chopped in a longish crew cut that surprisingly flattered her pert face. Skintight jeans and a baggy sweatshirt covered her compact body, and dark smudges stood out under her thick-lashed, sky blue eyes.

"David?" Her voice cracked as she spotted him. "Why have they dragged you down here?"

"I came of my own accord." He wanted to snatch the words back the second they left his mouth. Kollecki had warned him not to discuss the rose with anyone, and here he was blurting out that he'd come to the police station of his own volition. He blew out a flustered breath and lied. "To see if I could find out anything more than was in the newspaper."

"I'm waiting to see Detective Tagg." Denise took another drag on her cigarette. "Did they tell you anything?"

"Nope."

She blew out the smoke, blinking furiously, something another woman might do to keep tears at bay. But Denise claimed she didn't possess "fluffy female frailties." Like crying. He suspected the truth was that instead of acknowledging her feelings, she stifled them, a dangerous kind of repression that too often found negative outlets.

"You expect people to die." If she felt any pain, her voice didn't betray it. "It's part of life. I deal with it week in and week out. But someone you know being murdered is so...'Twilight Zone.'"

More than you know. David had a lump in his throat as big as the rose that now resided in Kollecki's property room.

The ash on the cigarette grew long as she leveled an odd gaze at him. "I didn't even know she was seeing this Prescott guy. Or that they were engaged. The only man Shan ever talked to me about was you."

He stiffened. "Then you know we were only friends." David pressed his lips together, his expression defying her to challenge his claim. Had Denise told Kollecki differently? Was she his source? "Have you spoken to Detective Kollecki?"

"Oh, him! Wouldn't tell me squat. But between you and me, my money's on that wife of Prescott's."

Without thought of the fallout it might incur, David leapt to Eden's defense. "Eden isn't capable of committing murder."

Denise glanced sharply at him. "Sounds like she's got a champion."

"Not really." David felt his face redden at the lie. "I've gotten to know her because of her sister. Beth Montgomery."

"I know whose sister she is. Friend of mine is Beth's live-in nurse." She lifted one eyebrow pointedly at him. "Has the widow Prescott ever rented your couch?"

"No." A nerve jumped in David's temple. "Eden's never been my patient."

Denise dropped her cigarette and ground it out with her boot. "Well then, maybe you don't know her as well as you think you do, David."

David curbed his rising temper, offered Denise his condolences, then excused himself and headed to his car. She was overcome with grief, frantic for answers, talking nonsense. He *did* know Eden. Knew her well. But what if Denise had spouted her slanted views to Kollecki?

He started his car engine and pulled out of his parking space. Too often in murder cases, the police had only to look to the victim's spouse for their perpetrator. Was that what had panicked Eden? The fear that she might soon be arrested?

He could only hope the rose had made a difference. Perhaps thrown another light on the evidence, diverted the focus from Eden, given the detectives something else to think about, someone else to look at.

Had he just sacrificed himself in the name of love?

Fear filtered through his thoughts and pulled a realization from some dark, hidden corner: what if this really wasn't about Peter Prescott but about Shannon? About some "source" who was under the misapprehension that she had been "special" to him? Was he crazy to think that? Egomaniacal? Given his experiences last February, he didn't think so.

He wished he'd told Eden about the rose before he'd handed it over to Kollecki, but he'd wanted to spare her extra worry. On the other hand, it might have eased her mind to know there was more going on than met the eye. And now the detective had cautioned him not to tell anyone about the rose. Well, the hell with Kollecki.

Eden and he needed to compare notes. Maybe with pooled information, they could figure out what was going on. Driving back to Seattle, he dialed her number and again got the answering machine. He kept phoning all afternoon, between classes and sessions with patients, and later at home. Finally after eight that evening, someone answered.

"Hello?" The voice was very like Eden's but without the strength.

"Beth?" he asked.

"Yeah...?" Wariness laced her tone. "Dr. Coulter?"

"Yes. How are you feeling, Beth?"

"Sad." To his trained ear, she sounded exhausted, but he knew part of that was the anemia. She asked, "Are you coming over?"

"Maybe. Is Eden there?"

"Sure. Eden! Telephone."

He heard Eden in the background. "Beth, I thought we agreed to let the machine pick up calls. I don't want to talk to any reporter—"

"It's not a reporter. It's Dr. Coulter."

There was a rustle of movement, then a long pause. "Eden?"

"Yes?" She sounded as if he'd startled her.

"Are you all right?" His grip tightened on the receiver.

"I've been better." She gave a nervous laugh.

"Beth sounds anxious...and exhausted."

"Right on both counts." Eden glanced at her sister. Beth's face, a younger version of her own, was ghostly white and pinched with strain. Her raven hair brushed her shoulders, limp and lackluster, and her cornflower blue eyes looked sunken.

"Would you like me to come over?" David asked.

Eden's pulse quickened. The memory of his gentle lovemaking sent delicious shudders through her, and two seconds passed before she regained her composure. She *did* want to talk to him, but not under Valerie's watchful eye. "That's not . . . a good idea."

"Is Valerie home?"

"Yes."

Another long pause ensued.

"Eden, about our talk . . . where and when?"

"I'm not sure." If only she could unload her conscience now, over the phone. Make him understand she hadn't really wished Peter would drop dead, hadn't meant she'd orchestrate any such an action. She wanted to tell him what she'd decided after she'd left his house—before she'd found out about Peter—and question him about Shannon, warn him that the police might consider him a suspect.

The knot in her stomach tightened. But just how wise was their meeting somewhere? What if the police were watching her at this very minute, or having her followed, or tapping her telephone?

"Why not here?" David sounded impatient at her silence. "Tonight?"

Beth moved closer, her look of eagerness dissolving into one of curiosity. The palms of Eden's hands were damp, slick on the receiver. She turned away and lowered her voice. "I just don't know."

"I'll be home all night."

Valerie walked into the kitchen. Eden's uneasiness bounced with new life. "I have to go."

She hung up. Beth asked, "Is he coming over?"

"He, who?" Valerie inquired.

Eden cringed, certain her sister would blurt out David's name, but Beth's nurse, Ariel Bell, saved the moment.

"It's nearly eight-thirty, Beth." Ariel was nearing her thirtieth birthday but had the kind of face that would always look ten years younger—not as much pretty as it was precious. She wore her sandy blond hair mid-length in an unkempt style, her large gray eyes barely visible through a tangle of uneven bangs. A hot-pink uniform pantsuit accented her slender legs, hugged her voluptuous breasts. "I've got your bath ready."

Beth took a warm bath before bed each night. She nodded at Ariel. "You won't get any complaints from me tonight. I'm beat."

The second Beth and Ariel were gone, Valerie turned back to Eden. She seemed about to pursue the "He, who?" issue again, but the doorbell rang. Eden started. Valerie jerked around, the phone conversation forgotten. Annoyance colored her pale cheeks, and a curse formed on her pinched lips. "If that's another reporter—"

The press had been relentless. Valerie's nerves had to be as ragged as her own. Eden took a calming breath as the ringing became more insistent. "Maybe we should let it ring, Val."

"Humph." Valerie spun on her heel and, taking long strides, headed for the door. Rolling her eyes, Eden followed her into the foyer. Valerie peered through the peephole. "For the love of—it's that horrid policeman again."

"Kollecki?" Eden's stomach crawled into her throat. What did he want now?

Valerie yanked open the door and addressed the man in clipped tones. "Detective. Have you figured out who killed my brother yet?" She glanced over her shoulder at Eden. "Or perhaps you've come to arrest one of us?"

Eden held her temper and her tongue.

"Not yet, ma'am," Kollecki said.

Valerie's chin came up. "Then what do you want?"

"We'd like to have a look around your house, if you wouldn't mind."

"Look around my—? You mean search it?" Incredulity rang in her voice. Valerie stepped back, her body as stiff as a pole. "But Peter wasn't killed here."

"Just the same..." Kollecki's words had an oily quality, slick and persistent.

A chill raced across Eden. Once, when she was thirteen, someone had broken into their apartment and gone through all the drawers, leaving her feeling violated. Even now, the thought of someone pawing through her clothing appalled her, but what it would do to Beth was worse. She moved into the detective's view. He nodded in greeting, but there was nothing friendly in the hard set of his mouth.

She felt as if he were pushing her into a corner. Irked, she lifted her chin and returned his measured gaze. "Do you have a search warrant?"

"Do I need one?" Kollecki asked evenly, but there was ice in his tone.

Tension hung like a pall between them.

"Oh, really." Valerie shook her head, lifting her hands in a dismissive gesture. "That isn't necessary, Eden."

"Yes, it is. This is my home, too, Val. I don't want Beth upset unnecessarily. And strangers in the house digging through drawers and cupboards will make her more anxious than she already is tonight.''

Valerie shrugged, lifting her ginger-colored brows in concession. "She's right, Detective. Beth *is* fragile and she's terribly anxious today. She's about to go to bed. Perhaps you could come tomorrow? That would give us time to prepare the poor dear.''

Kollecki glanced at Eden, one brow arched as he awaited her answer to this suggestion. She sighed. "All right. Tomorrow morning. But not before ten.''

"Have it your way." A muscle twitched in his jaw, and the look in his eyes sent a dagger of fear through Eden's heart. Once again she saw that he thought *she* had killed Peter and Shannon Smalley.

The second Kollecki left, Eden fled to her bedroom. But a hot bath did nothing to ease her distress. With pressure tightening her chest, she donned jeans, a lightweight sweater and loafers, grabbed her keys, and—vaguely noting Valerie's Mercedes was gone from the garage—got behind the wheel of her minivan.

THE WOMAN PARKED her car one house away from David's. Excitement and anticipation heated her blood and filled her senses, almost blocking out the aroma wafting from the sacks of Chinese takeout on the passenger seat. If the way to a man's heart was through his stomach, David's heart was all but hers. She'd bought his favorites. Including the cabernet he loved.

And one single red rose. Red was for love. And she did love David.

Poor man. He'd been terribly upset today. Not that she'd have expected otherwise. A smile parted her lips. She'd caused his distress; it was only fair she ease it. Of course, he'd be glad to see her. He needed her comfort.

And with Shannon out of the way, he'd start seeing how much he needed her love. How much they belonged together.

For they did belong together.

They shared the same taste for many things. Like combs. She reached into the glove box and lifted one free; it still contained strands of his chocolate brown hair. Precious strands. She kissed the comb, then set it back in the glove box beside the others she'd taken out of his bathroom over the past two months. Had he missed them? Just in case, she'd take something different tonight.

She reached for the sacks of food. There remained a few minor obstacles to overcome, but soon she'd have won David's love and secured their future. A happy sigh escaped her. They were going to have the most beautiful children together. Lots of children.

She gripped the door handle, glanced toward his house and froze. Eden was knocking on David's door. With shock and disbelief, the woman watched David open the door, watched him pull Eden into his arms.

Stunned, the woman flopped back against the seat. What was going on? When had *she* started making moves on David? She'd only lost her husband last night. Anger, red and hot as lava, spurted through the woman's veins.

Has this been going on for a while now? Right under my nose? She could think of no other explanation. Her sob of outrage and pain resounded inside the car. Another adversary. She dropped the sacks of food to the seat beside the bottle of wine, smashing the rose as flat as her hopes.

But her depression was short-lived. She spotted Eden's minivan across the street, and an idea struck her.

An idea with great potential. Her confidence surged with new energy. She was getting quite expert at annihilating her competition for David's affection. The woman got out of the car and went around to her trunk. Eden was all but gone.

Chapter Four

David ushered Eden into his kitchen. It was a square-shaped room with a center island that held the stove and sink on one side and an eating counter opposite. Black and white tiles checkered the floor and countertops, softened by the white appliances and warmed by the chili-pepper red bar stools, miniblinds and hanging light fixtures.

Eden scrambled onto one of the stools. "Something smells wonderful."

"Heating cinnamon rolls and fresh Starbucks coffee." David could feel the tension issuing from her, and before he brought up the murders, he wanted to put her at ease. "The rolls will be ready soon. Coffee?"

Eden nodded. He poured them each a cup and slid onto the bar stool beside hers, leaning his elbow on the counter.

She reached for the mug. "Do you serve hot cinnamon rolls to all your guests?"

"I find an occasional shot of sugar is good for the soul." Grinning wryly, he gazed into her eyes, and the memory of their lovemaking swept through his head, a whispery shadow on the edges of his mind, teasing him, haunting him, stirring renewed need. "I'm glad you changed your mind about coming over."

Eden took a gulp of coffee and set the mug down shakily. "Kollecki changed my mind."

David straightened in his seat but checked the alarm he felt before it could reveal itself in his expression. "How did he do that?"

"He showed up shortly after we spoke."

"Why?" David sipped his coffee. "What did he want?"

"To search the house." She gazed up at him. "He thinks I killed Shannon Smalley and Peter."

"No." Hearing his greatest fear put into words sent a bolt of panic through David. "I hoped after I took him the rose, he'd—"

"The rose?"

"Let's take our coffee into the living room and get comfortable." He stood. "We have some information to share."

Eden lurched off the stool. Her heel caught in the rung, and she pitched against David, her nose coming to rest inches from his solid chest. She drew a quavery breath, pulling in the clean smell of him. His heart was thudding against her palms.

Slowly she lifted her gaze and found herself staring into his moss green eyes. Blood burned through her veins, speeding heat to every pore, to every sensitive nerve ending.

Levering the heels of her hands against his flat, muscled midriff, she attempted to right herself, but she couldn't pull loose from the smoldering look in David's eyes. He grasped her elbows and drew her up and against him, his head lowering until his mouth hovered a breath away from hers.

"Oh, David, I'm so scared."

"I know, my love." He claimed her mouth in a kiss that was fierce and feverish and feral, the kiss of a man who had finally found the woman he'd longed for, a kiss that curled tendrils of pleasure through Eden and stole the fear from her thoughts.

The smoke alarm bleated. They jerked apart. Smoke stole from the closed oven door.

David shouted, "The rolls!"

Eden tossed him an oven mitt and stood back as he threw open the oven door. Smoke billowed out and into the room, racing toward the ceiling. David extracted the cookie sheet and deposited it in the sink. The thick, gooey rolls he had put in the oven were now small, blackened pinwheels.

Laughing for the first time in days, Eden yelled above the alarm, "I think you'd better stick to psychiatry."

Also laughing, David turned off the oven and opened the window. "As opposed to being an arsonist?"

"Being a chef." She ran cold water over the cookie sheet, sending a curtain of steam to join the smoke near the ceiling.

David deactivated the annoying alarm, then stepped behind her and kissed the nape of her neck. "How about if I stick to being your lover?"

Eden spun slowly in his arms. "Now, there's a plan."

She pulled his head to hers, and their lips met, tentatively, then with confidence and need. David lifted her and carried her to his bed. The room was like David, soft greens and browns, with a rumpled kind of warmth and an innate cleanliness.

His pillows smelled of his spicy after-shave, and the moment he joined her on the bed, Eden was lost in the joy of his touch, in the joy of touching. This time there was no hurry to their lovemaking, but a languid exploring, a sweet acquainting of bodies, a honeyed pleasuring, a release of feelings long denied.

Afterward David rolled to his side and pulled Eden against him. "I wish we could stay like this forever."

"I do, too." Eden's body felt aglow, the sensation new and prized. She propped herself on one elbow and gazed into David's eyes. "But I think Kollecki has a different agenda in mind for me."

A slight trembling stole over her, and she couldn't hide the apprehension from him. David scooted up against the headboard and dragged the sheet over them. "Kollecki is one of the things I wanted to discuss."

Eden sat up and hugged her knees, glancing sideways at him. "Do you know a good lawyer? Jacoby and Otterman, Peter's lawyers, are corporate attorneys. I need a criminal lawyer."

David wanted to protest, to declare she needed no such thing, but he knew better. Kollecki could be ruthless in the pursuit of justice and if he decided she was the murderer, she'd better have the best legal counsel she could hire. "I don't know any personally, but tomorrow I'll make some discreet inquiries. Eden, tell me everything you know about Peter and Shannon's murders."

"Why?" She looked affronted, as if he were questioning her innocence.

Deep down, David knew he was. He'd misjudged people before, trusted when he shouldn't have. As much as he wanted to believe Eden, the only way to silence the niggling doubts was to hear the truth. He reached up and gently grazed his knuckles along her jawline. "Because if this lawyer is going to get you off, he needs all the information related to the case, not just Kollecki's version."

"What do you want to know?"

"Everything that happened the day of the murders. Anything else that seems pertinent. I have a few things to tell you, too."

He could see her trust in him return. He wished his own trust was as solid. She told him every detail she could recall leading up to Peter's storming out of the house, the few things she'd gleaned from the detectives and finally what she'd overheard about Shannon and him.

In turn David related the facts of Marianne De-Paul's case as he knew them, as much as he could recall about Rose Hatcher—including a physical description—and finally about the rose left for him that morning.

Her eyes rounded at this last, and she stiffened. "But if you're right, you could be in danger."

Realization slammed into David. "Dear God, if I'm right, _you're_ the one in danger."

The color left Eden's face, and she clenched her hands together as if to keep them from trembling. "The police or a killer... How did my life come to this awful place?"

David reached for the bedside phone and began dialing. "I'm telling Kollecki about us. He can have you guarded around the clock."

"No!" Eden lunged across David and aborted the call. " 'Us' only makes me look more guilty. Kollecki won't believe anyone is after me. Even if he did, he doesn't have the manpower to offer me protection."

He lurched off the bed and began dressing. "Then I'll hire you a bodyguard."

"And how would that look to Kollecki?" Eden donned her underwear and tugged on her jeans. "I can hire my own bodyguard."

David stood. "I'll get the phone book. You can call now."

"David, I appreciate your desire to protect me, but nothing is going to happen to me between here and Issaquah. I'll call from home." She pulled her sweater over her head and glanced at the digital clock on the nightstand. "Speaking of which, I'd better get back before Valerie realizes I'm gone and does something dumb."

At the foyer, she stopped David from going outside with her. "Except where Beth is concerned, we can't be seen together until this case is solved."

David knew she was right. "But I'm going to walk you to your van."

"No. Even that could be dangerous. I didn't catch anyone following me from home, but I wouldn't put it past Kollecki to have a tail on me."

David shuddered inwardly. If the rose had any significance, they had more to worry about than Kollecki. The fear of losing Eden overwhelmed him. "I don't want to let you go."

"I don't want to go, but I must."

She kissed him goodbye before he opened the door, and insisted he turn off the foyer light and leave the porch light off. She stepped gingerly outside, reassured that David watched from the open doorway.

As she hurried across the street to the van, she scanned the road for any vehicle that seemed occupied or out of place. Nothing untoward caught her eye. It seemed like any other peaceful Northwest neighborhood on a cool July night.

Breathing easier, she slid the key into the lock. Alarm chilled her. The door was not locked. Her heart picked up speed. She yanked open the door. The interior light blinked on, glaringly bright in her fear. Hating its prolonged exposure of her, she checked behind the back seat and into the rear recesses of the van. No one lurked inside. Nothing seemed amiss. Her breath sputtered out.

She plopped into the driver's seat and hit her door latch. Hadn't she locked the van when she'd arrived? It was something she did automatically. Had she been that upset by Kollecki that she'd forgotten? That anxious to see David again?

Recalling that he was watching from his doorway and probably wondering what was causing the delay in her departure, she willed herself to be calm. She shoved the key in the ignition. Would loving David cost her her life? It was a gruesome thought. She turned the key. The engine revved.

Eden spent anxious minutes reaching the Issaquah Plateau, constantly searching the rearview mirror for signs that someone was following. The tension gripping her eased as she pulled into her housing development. Then she spotted her house. She'd expected everyone would be in bed, the house dark. Instead, every light in the place burned brightly.

A patrol car and an unmarked car she recognized as Kollecki's were parked out front. Fear dampened her palms and prickled her scalp. She parked in the garage and locked the van, double-checking to be certain before heading into the house.

In the kitchen, Valerie, Beth and Ariel were seated at the table. All were white-faced and anxious. Valerie explained, "They came back . . . with a warrant."

"Pulled Beth right out of a sound sleep. Not so much as an 'I'm sorry,' either," Ariel complained. "I'm not used to working under these conditions. It's not good for my patient."

"It's not good for any of us, Ariel," Eden assured the nurse. "Are you okay, Beth?"

Beth nodded but she looked more pale than usual. Kollecki had some explaining to do. Dropping her keys into her purse, Eden searched for and found him in her bedroom. Dresser drawers hung open, clothing, intimate apparel and all, trailing over the edges like loose stuffing pulled from a chair, her worst nightmare come true. She tamped down her anger, but her words came out clipped. "You promised you'd wait until tomorrow."

"I promised no such thing."

She started to protest and realized the futility of it. He hadn't said he'd wait; he'd said, "Have it your way," which apparently meant that he'd objected to her resistance and decided to have it *his* way. But what did they expect to find?

She returned to the kitchen, poured herself some coffee, then strode to the table. As she was about to sit, Ariel reached out and grabbed at something that had apparently stuck to the seat of her jeans. "What's this?"

Eden frowned at the small white object Ariel held, half expecting it to be a feather from David's down comforter, but the shape and texture were wrong.

Valerie said, "Looks like part of a flower."

Ariel brought it to her nose. "Rose petal."

A chill shot through Eden. She dropped into the chair, sloshing coffee onto the tabletop.

"What's wrong, Eden?" Beth's eyes rounded in alarm.

Eden realized she was scaring her sister even more than the police were. She forced a placid expression onto her face. "Nothing, hon. Don't worry. This is just routine in a murder investigation. They'll be gone soon, and everything will be back to normal."

Beth seemed to take some comfort in the explanation. Eden wished she could, but her mind was racing. How had a white rose petal gotten stuck to her jeans? Had she picked it up from David's house? Or from her van?

"Just where have you been the past few hours, Eden?" Valerie inquired.

Eden flushed, remembering. "I was driving."

Kollecki strolled into the kitchen. "Seems you have a propensity for driving. Haven't you heard about conserving gas?"

Before Eden could respond to that, a uniformed policeman rushed in from the garage. He was young and excited and clutched a long, slender tool that looked like something used to open locked cars. Eden's skin prickled.

The young man addressed Kollecki. "I was just coming to get you, sir. You'll want to see this."

As they headed back into the garage, Eden noticed her van door was open and that another uniformed policeman was standing near it. Her heart jumped to an explosive beat. She lurched to her feet and hurried into the garage behind Kollecki.

He bent down, craned his neck sideways, tugged a pencil from his pocket, poked it beneath the driver's seat and lifted something out.

"What is it?" Her voice was a breathless rasp.

Kollecki stretched to his full height and held out the object so she could see it. A gun. "I'm betting we just found the murder weapon."

Chapter Five

Six weeks later

In the privacy of her bedroom, the woman laid the *Seattle Times* on her dresser drawer and read the front-page article with relish. Six wonderful weeks ago, Eden Prescott had been arrested. The paper crinkled as the woman folded it to an inside page. It did her heart good to picture Eden sitting in a dingy jail cell. No bail for her.

She'd been charged and arraigned for first-degree murder. Satisfaction wound through the woman. If all went as it should, prosecutors would seek the death penalty.

Talk about fifteen minutes of fame. Eden had gotten more than her due so far. The media had fed on the story like a frenzy of bloodthirsty sharks. It was all anyone talked about lately, and everyone had the same opinion: Eden Prescott was guilty as sin.

The woman laughed gleefully. Control. That was where the power was. Men knew it. Learned it before kindergarten, she suspected. Well, she'd learned it now. "Oh, yeah. I am a force to be reckoned with."

The woman glanced up from the paper and across to the brass-framed photograph of David. She jammed her hand through her hair as a sigh rushed from that tiny part of her that felt sorry for him. He was so obviously distressed about Eden. The woman laughed again. Bitterly this time. Mostly David deserved every agonizing minute that he suffered; it was just payment for his involvement with that Jezebel.

He'd even found her a high-clout lawyer—some guy from Arizona whom the press likened to a young Gerry Spence with his fringed buckskin jacket and black shirts. Seemed he was as clever as Mr. Spence, too.

A tiny worry threatened to push past her confidence. She shoved it away. Clever or not, that lawyer wasn't going to get the case thrown out at the evidentiary hearing tomorrow. The evidence was too strong.

The woman reached into the vase of white roses behind David's photograph, drew one out and inhaled its delicate fragrance. Not only had the police found the murder weapon in Eden's possession, but—as luck would have it—her fingerprints were also on the gun.

"DAMMIT KOLLECKI, I don't care if you did find the murder weapon in Eden's van!" David's throat constricted at the anger and frustration boiling inside him. "The damned thing belongs to Valerie! Eden and she have lived in the same house for seven years. She could have touched that gun any time during those years. You have no way of telling how old fingerprints are."

"Calm down, Dr. Coulter." Kollecki looked up from his position behind his desk, his dark eyes narrowed like those of a coiled snake. "Or this meeting is over."

"How am I supposed to calm down when someone keeps leaving these on my doorstep?" With his chest heaving as it did after a five-mile jog, David slapped another Ziploc bag—with yet another rose inside— down onto Kollecki's desk. Just looking at it filled his gut with icy fear. His first instinct had been to grind it to a pulp, but then he'd realized the significance of it. "This was on my doorstep this morning."

Kollecki's tense demeanor relaxed a modicum. He contemplated the rose, then eyed David with suspicion. "What's that make—two now?"

"Yes!" Was Kollecki finally getting it?

"So what? No one died this time."

Impotent rage cracked like a whip inside David. "You're not a stupid man." He struggled to control his temper, but his voice rose an octave. "Why do you refuse to see the significance of this? The killer thinks she's eliminated Eden as effectively as if she'd murdered her."

The expression on Kollecki's face reminded David of one he'd often given to overwrought patients. It jarred him to his toes. If he didn't calm down, Kollecki would listen to nothing he had to say. But he hadn't had a calm bone in his body since the day Eden had been arrested.

Kollecki angled back in his chair, evidently taking David's momentary silence as an attempt at composure.

"Contrary to some of the crap you see on TV or read in books, Doctor, we don't arrest people without due cause." Kollecki planted his elbows on his desk and began ticking off points with his fingers. "First there was the divorce, which legally—thanks to the prenuptial agreement she signed—would leave Mrs. Prescott without much more than the few dollars she had coming into the marriage."

"Eden doesn't care about money."

"Maybe not for herself. But Prescott was dropping her sister and her from his medical-insurance policy, and we both know that meant her sister would not be able to pay for the kidney transplant she so desperately needs."

David swallowed over the lump in his throat.

"Second, Valerie Prescott reported her gun missing three weeks before the murders. Someone in that house had to have taken it. Third—"

"You didn't even read the report she filed about the gun, did you?"

Kollecki puffed out his cheeks.

David thumped his desk. "If you had, you'd know the gun was stolen from her car. With the news full of car-jackings, Valerie started carrying it in her Mercedes' glove box. She bragged to everyone about it, including my office staff. Anyone could have taken it."

Kollecki didn't even blink. "*Third,* Mrs. Prescott cannot account for her whereabouts at the crucial time. Motive, means and opportunity. She did it."

"No. She didn't," David said in a voice as tight as his hands at his sides. Heat climbed his neck. "*I* can account for her whereabouts at the crucial time."

Kollecki sighed impatiently. "I'm listening."

"She was with me until after nine o'clock."

"Nine o'clock, huh?" The detective steepled his fingertips. "That's interesting. You live on Mercer Island, right?"

David nodded.

"And Smalley and Prescott were killed at her house—which is what? Max, some twenty, twenty-five minutes away?" Kollecki smirked. "More than enough time to drive from your place to the murder scene."

David dropped into the chair across from Kollecki. He was getting nowhere. He had always known it was physically possible for Eden to have committed the crime, had even struggled with doubts over her guilt, but dammit, she couldn't have left the roses. Especially the second one—she was in jail. And the roses had to mean something.

But shouting would never convince Kollecki of what David knew deep down inside: no matter what the evidence was, no matter how strong Eden's motives were, she could not kill another human being. He took several deep breaths, reaching into that part of himself where he'd stowed his ability to reason in a calm and forthright manner. At length he said, "Kollecki, how can I convince you that Eden isn't the kind of person who commits murder?"

Kollecki's eyes held pity. "Do you realize, Doctor, you said the exact same thing about Rose Hatcher?"

Almost word for word, David recalled, feeling sick to his stomach. Was he wrong about Eden as he had been about Rose Hatcher? He considered Detective Tagg's suggestion about a copycat killer. Was there one? Or was Rose Hatcher actually innocent? Would an innocent woman confess to murder? He gripped the arms of the chair with whitened knuckles.

"It was a nice try, Doc."

David glanced sharply at Kollecki. "What?"

"You know...the roses. Trying to raise reasonable doubt for your girlfriend."

David shook his head. "No, I—"

"It wouldn't have worked. She did it."

No. The word died in his throat. Why waste the breath? Kollecki's mind was set as hard as concrete. *Hell, he pities me. Well, I don't need his damned pity.*

He bit down his anger. Maybe he could make use of Kollecki's pity. "Can you arrange for me to see Eden?"

The detective pressed his lips together, considering. David heard his own breath, noisy in the heavy silence. "It wasn't that tough a question, Kollecki."

"Why don't you cut your losses?"

David's temper rose another notch. "Today."

"Maybe after the 3.5 hearing."

David guessed a 3.5 hearing was the evidentiary hearing that was set for the following day at the King County Courthouse in downtown Seattle. He intended to be present while lawyers for both sides argued the evidence in this case. Worry nagged him. Would the judge decide there was enough hard evidence to go to trial?

"That's tomorrow. Why make me wait another day?"

"The hearing was rescheduled for this morning."

"What?" David started up from the chair. "When?"

"You'll never make it, Doc. It started two hours ago. Probably over." Kollecki gestured to someone who was apparently standing outside his office peering in through the windowed door, waiting to enter. "In fact, it must be."

David shifted around as Detective Tagg entered the office, leaving the door agape. He was dressed in a suit and tie and wore a dejected look on his narrow features. Had Tagg been to the hearing in Seattle?

Kollecki frowned. "What's the matter?"

"You aren't going to like it. The judge threw out our case against the Prescott woman."

David's heart leapt into his throat. Did that mean what it sounded like it meant?

"No!" Kollecki was on his feet. "Not because—"

"Yep."

"Damned rookie!" Kollecki slammed his fist on the desk. His face was as red as his hair. He glared at David. "Looks like you'll be able to see your girlfriend *at home* this afternoon."

David was too stunned to do anything but stare back. Kollecki stormed out of the room. David staggered to his feet, afraid to hope he was hearing right. "Will somebody tell me what the hell is going on? Is Eden free?"

"Yes." Tagg sighed. "The judge ruled her Fourth Amendment rights were violated in the procurement of the gun."

Free. Eden was free. He was afraid to believe it. "But you had a search warrant—how were her rights violated?"

Tagg loosened his tie and undid the top button of his shirt. "We found the gun under the driver's seat of her van, but because the van was locked, we had no right to enter it without permission from her—unless the warrant so stated, which it didn't."

Kollecki returned, his face still an unhealthy crimson. "In other words, since the gun is the primary evidence linking Mrs. Prescott to the crime, and since it was procured in an illegal manner, it cannot be used as evidence against her."

"Accordingly all charges were dropped." Tagg's bushy gray eyebrows twitched as he noticed the rose for the first time. He glanced questioningly at his partner, then back at David. But neither satisfied his unspoken curiosity.

David felt as if the weight of the world had been wrenched from him. Joy ran through his veins, sang in his ears. He all but shouted, "I told you she was innocent."

Kollecki's eyes narrowed into thin black slits. "Don't misunderstand, Doctor. Mrs. Prescott hasn't been found innocent. There's no statute of limitations on murder. When we discover new evidence, she can and will be arrested and charged again."

"There's no evidence to find, Kollecki. Why don't you follow up on the roses?"

"Roses? Plural?" Tagg stepped to the desk and grasped the Ziploc bag. The rose inside was not crushed as the other had been. He gazed at David.

"Yes," David confirmed. "A second one. I found it this morning. While Mrs. Prescott was in custody."

"What's it mean?" Tagg asked his partner.

Kollecki scowled at David. "Nothing."

David growled in frustration. Kollecki had convinced himself Eden was guilty, and that was that. He would stick to this case like a hound after a rabbit, never believing he was on the wrong scent. "You're making a grave mistake, Kollecki."

David started toward the door, hesitated and glanced at the more reasonable Tagg. "You've got an open mind. Try and talk some sense into your partner... before another innocent woman is murdered."

With that, he left.

At long last, she was free. But his admonition to the detectives haunted him. Eden was the innocent woman he was worried about. With the police determined to see her as the killer instead of a possible next victim, she was in dire jeopardy. Somehow he had to discover who was leaving the roses.

But first he had to warn Eden.

EDEN LOWERED her weary body into the bubble-filled bathtub. She breathed in the sweet-scented steam rising from the water, relishing the privacy of her own bathroom, a privacy she thought she'd never know again.

She had arrived home to news cars and trucks— bearing logos from local and national newspaper, radio and television stations—camped in front of the house. The second she stepped from her attorney's car, reporters besieged her. The lawyer hustled her through the maze, spouting something about his client being innocent and the judge having the good sense to uphold justice.

Justice? Eden almost laughed. But the situation wasn't funny. The stress of this ordeal showed in Beth's drawn face and her weakened condition. How much more could she take? Ariel had confided that her condition was worsening, that Beth was running out of veins for the dialysis. If a donor wasn't found soon...

No. She would not think negatively. She was free. She ought to be celebrating. That did pull a laugh from her. Celebrating indeed. She'd run straight in here and heaved up the small amount of food she'd managed to get down this morning. Oddly her stomach was still upset, an awful queasiness akin to the nauseous sensation she felt whenever she attempted boating.

In some distant recess of the house, she could hear the telephone ringing. The answering machine would pick it up. She didn't care who it was—maybe "Hard Copy" or "Inside Edition" again. As if she'd talk to any of those people. She reached for the bath sponge, lathered it with perfumed soap and, starting with her feet, scrubbed with all her might.

The media had already tried and convicted her, smug in their predictions of the verdict. They hadn't gotten the outcome they'd wanted. Neither had she. Pulling in a deep breath, she sank completely beneath the water's surface. The silence was as blessed as if she'd stepped into a world free of chaos, as if she were sheathed in a warm cocoon.

But as she emerged and took in a gulp of air, reality wrapped her in its chilly cloak. She was innocent, but the judge hadn't verified that innocence. He'd condemned her to being thought of forever as a murderer.

She turned on the faucet, dipped her head under the clear water, rinsed the soap from her hair, then shut off the faucet and scraped the dripping hair back from her eyes. What was she going to do? How could she go on in this community, this state, being scorned, gossiped about, stared at, thought guilty of the heinous crime of double murder?

She rested her head against the bath pillow and stared at the burgundy-and-gray mosaic design on the tile above the faucets. Who *had* murdered Peter and Shannon? Who had planted the gun in her van? Cold fear landed like a chunk of ice in her unsettled stomach. She closed her eyes and swallowed hard to keep the nausea at bay.

She'd had six long weeks to think about who was the real killer. Time and again, these deliberations brought Valerie to mind. The gun was hers. Planting it in the van would have been easy for Val. But why would she kill Peter, the brother she loved to distraction?

Eden blew out a wobbly breath. Just how mentally stable was Val? Why had David counseled her? Had it had something to do with Peter? Eden considered. Val's love for her brother had been a bit overboard. And unrequited. By falling in love with Shannon, Peter had once again rejected Val. Had that been enough to send her over the brink of sanity?

Eden set the sponge aside. That such a thought could even occur to her meant that Beth and she had to leave this house. But where could they go? Out of this town. This state. She sat straighter in the tub, feeling suddenly as trapped as if she were once again behind bars. The transplant. Beth had to be near the hospital in case a kidney became available.

Until then, she *was* trapped.

But the first moment after surgery that Beth was well enough to travel, they would disappear, even change their names.

What about David?

The thought hit her like a blow to the chest, an ache so strong it felt as if a hole the size of a fist had pierced her heart. She whispered, "Oh, David. I do love you."

And right now she needed him so.

The soft sound of the bedroom door opening and closing reached through the open bathroom door, startling Eden out of her reverie. She jumped. Water sloshed the edges of the tub. Goose bumps lifted on her warm skin. She'd given Valerie, Ariel and Beth strict instructions not to disturb her. No matter what.

Had one of them ignored her orders? Or had some enterprising reporter breached their security? Then again, maybe it was the killer. Once more her suspicion of Valerie loomed. Fear climbed into her throat. Her gaze riveted on the half-open bathroom door, she reached for a towel and started to stand.

"Eden, it's me. David."

Relief flooded through her, bringing the first pleasant quickening of her heart in weeks. She'd never been so glad to hear someone's voice. She stepped onto the bath mat and wrapped the huge towel around herself, calling out, "Give me a couple of minutes."

Quickly she dried and dressed in a silk pantsuit, then began combing her hair. It needed cutting. She blanched at the thought of calling Cheré for an appointment. With a sinking heart, Eden realized there was probably not a salon in town she could patronize without being recognized.

Anger flared inside her, burning away all the self-pity she'd been feeling. Dammit. She was innocent. There had to be some way of proving it. But every possible course of action that occurred to her as she smoothed on lipstick seemed dangerous and foolhardy.

If there were only herself to consider, she might try to draw her nemesis out into the open. But she couldn't put Beth at risk. Or David. The only thing that made any sense was to reiterate David's and her decision not to see one another anymore.

With a heavy heart, she left the bathroom. David, in white Dockers and a royal blue polo shirt, was a breath of fresh air in this room that reflected Peter's brooding personality and stilted tastes. He stood beside the dark pine dresser gazing at the framed photograph displayed there—a gathering of the Montgomery clan when she was still a child. It was all that remained of her family besides Beth and herself.

"Hello, David." Despite her mind-set, she wanted to run to him and throw her arms around him and lose herself in the security of his embrace. Instead, she strode to the chaise longue and laid her hands on its arched back.

He lurched around, a jerky, nervous movement. He looked as tired as she felt. Then he smiled, and a joyful light filled his eyes. "It's so wonderful to see you here instead..."

The sentence trailed off, and she knew he'd been about to add *instead of in jail*. She shifted from one foot to the other. "I was going to call you. To thank you...for the lawyer."

He made no move toward her, but she could see he wanted to. "I tried calling, but you weren't answering your phone. We have to talk."

Eden was too aware of where they were, of the others in the house. "Does Valerie know you're in my bedroom?"

He smirked. "She's not happy about it, but I insisted."

Eden winced, imagining the silent rage she would suffer from Valerie later.

"I figured this was the only way we'd have complete privacy." David took three steps toward her, then halted abruptly, as if held back by an invisible restraint. "I've just come from Kollecki's office."

"Oh?" Inexplicably she shivered.

"I found another white rose on my doorstep this morning."

Eden grasped the back of the chaise, its wine red brocade fabric feeling icy beneath her taut fingers. "I don't understand. Who is sending them to you? And why?"

"I have a theory as to why I received this one, if you'd like to hear it."

"Please." She glanced down. A thread had pulled loose at the seam of the chaise, unraveling as her life seemed to be unraveling.

David ached to rush to her and fold her against him, but it would be madness. Fatal, even. Swallowing over the lump in his throat that he suspected might be his breaking heart, he watched Eden pick at the loose thread. She'd had enough pain the past six weeks to bring down the hardiest soul. She had to be on the edge of coming apart. It made what he had to say so much harder. He kept his voice gentle as he explained his theory of the woman thinking she'd gotten rid of Eden by framing her.

"What did Kollecki say about that?"

David shook his head. "He isn't taking the roses seriously."

Eden searched for the truth on David's face. "He's going to keep after me, isn't he?" Of course he was. Why should that surprise her? And yet somehow it did. Desperation and fear tangled inside her. And she'd been thinking the largest concern she faced in the days ahead was public scorn. "You believe Peter died because he was in the wrong place at the wrong time?"

"Yes. The roses confirm for me that Shannon was the real target. I think they were both killed because some woman thought Shannon and I were romantically involved." David took another step toward her. "That's why you have to stay as far away from me as possible."

His words hit her like tiny sharp stones. But hadn't she been going to say the same thing to him? Then why did it hurt so? She shoved away from the chaise and walked past him to the window. But she dared not look out. She turned and strode back to where he stood beside the four-poster bed. "Do you have any idea who this woman is?"

He thought again of Rose Hatcher. No. She was tucked safely away in Purdy, the state prison for women. "No clue."

A sob climbed Eden's throat. "This is awful. We don't even know who we're afraid of."

David moved closer. It was tearing him apart not to hold her. But he knew he wouldn't be able to walk out of here if he gave in to the potent urge. "Whoever she is, she needs help."

"David, are you sure you're not in danger?" Eden jammed her hands against her temples. Her head ached as if it might explode. "So much has happened to me in the past six weeks that I can't even sort out my feelings about most of it. But the one thing I'm very clear on is that I don't want anything to happen to you."

"I'll be fine. Ducking the dangers of obsessive disorders is something psychiatrists learn to deal with. Besides, obsessives usually follow a pattern." His tone was reassuring, but passion burned in his eyes—anger or frustration, perhaps both. "And her pattern seems to be eradicating the women from my life who she thinks are close to me. So it's damned likely she'll keep coming after you until she finishes what she started. You have to stay the hell away from me."

Eden knew she should be afraid. Deathly afraid. But she felt as if her heart were bleeding, pricked by the thorns of the white roses. She asked quietly, "Will this be forever?"

"No!" He closed the gap between them. "Only until she's caught."

His familiar, beloved scent reached into Eden, and she nearly took the single step that would bring them together. But she held herself rigid. "What if she's never caught?"

"She will be. No matter what it takes, *I* will unmask her."

The loathing in his voice surprised Eden. It was unlike him to express as much as an unkind thought about someone he considered ill. Her voice broke as she said, "I'll never forget what we had, David."

"It's not over, Eden." He caressed her cheek with his knuckles. "Just on hold."

But it was over. She knew it. Her stomach clenched, and her knees wobbled.

The bedroom door banged open. David and Eden started as if they'd been caught in bed instead of standing beside it. Valerie stood there, glaring at them. "Forgive my intrusion on your tender reunion."

Eden stepped around David, glad to have someone to vent her bottled-up frustrations on. "How dare you barge in here without knocking!"

Valerie looked affronted and hurt. "You're so ungrateful, Eden. I thought you'd want to know immediately. Beth's pager just went off. The hospital has a donor."

Chapter Six

Eden's pulse leapt, her anger at Valerie's intrusion fleeing on the wings of this wonderful news. "Is Ariel getting Beth ready to leave?"

"No." Valerie was suddenly flustered. "She doesn't even know about it yet. She had some errands that needed tending to, so I told her you and I would watch over Beth while she was out. I suppose we could leave her a note."

Valerie sounded as if she intended on going to the hospital; Eden wasn't certain she could deal with her in light of the suspicions she harbored. But how did she tell her without making an issue of it?

As if he sensed her dilemma, David said, "It isn't necessary for you to come to the hospital, Valerie. We won't know for a while whether or not there will even be any surgery."

It was amazing, Eden mused, how he kept being there for her. Then again, she supposed it shouldn't surprise her. His thoughtfulness had caused her to take her first good look at him six months ago, and was now only one of his many qualities she adored. But dwelling on her feelings for David would only break her heart.

Returning her attention to the situation, she realized Valerie was not convinced. Eden took a firmer stand. "I'll call you as soon as we know one way or the other."

Valerie's lips pinched, and her eyes glistened with anger. She opened her mouth, presumably to object, but Beth appeared in the doorway. "Eden, can you get my suitcase? Stupid thing feels like it weighs a ton."

Beth's complexion had a greenish gray cast, and her eyes held a mixture of relief and apprehension. Eden patted her arm reassuringly. "Of course. I'll meet you in the garage."

Eden brushed past Valerie and left the room. As she started down the hall, she heard Beth say, "You're coming with me, aren't you, Dr. Coulter?"

Despite his insistence that they avoid one another at all costs, Eden knew David would not abandon any patient in need. But as glad as she was at the prospect of not facing this alone, a part of her feared the killer would see them together and make wrong assumptions.

By the time she joined Beth and David in the kitchen, she felt her nerves fraying. Valerie hovered in a corner, resentment stark in her deep-set eyes. Was she only angry at being excluded? Or was she the woman they both feared? The thought swept over Eden like a chilly breeze. Val's love for her brother had been like that of an overly possessive mother. Did she love David in a different, yet similarly possessive way?

If I'm right, Eden realized, *the killer is here in this room with us, already watching, already making wrong assumptions, perhaps already plotting my demise.*

She set Beth's suitcase on the floor and pulled her key ring from her purse. It slipped from her trembling hand, falling to the floor with a jarring jangle.

At the same moment, David and she scrambled after the keys, their hands reaching out, their fingers colliding and their gazes meeting and holding. The warmth of his touch stirred a deep hunger in Eden.

"Hey, you two, can we get a move on?" Beth groused.

The blunt reminder that they were not alone heated Eden's cheeks. She straightened, leaving the keys to David. He said, "I'll drive."

"Thank you." She gave him a grateful smile, then she grimaced and hugged Beth around the shoulders. "I'm so excited for you, I've got the heebie-jeebies."

"I know what you mean." Beth's laugh held no strength and quickly died as Eden steered her to the garage.

Eden wished she could drive away from this house that held only unhappiness and fear for her now and never return. But she didn't want Beth sensing this negative mood.

She forced gaiety into her voice, spouting small talk to occupy Beth's mind, to stave off her own concerns that started with her sister's well-being and ended with a murderer.

Her stomach was still unsettled, but she noticed her gaiety wasn't all put on. Hope, she realized, was giving her a buoyant feeling. Hope, and David's presence and support. She helped Beth into the front passenger seat, then slid onto the bench seat behind David.

The moment the garage door began opening, they heard it—a swelling buzz of noise like a swarm of bees gearing up for attack. The reporters and camera people converged over the concrete driveway without heed that the van was rolling toward them. David honked the horn and kept backing out of the garage. Shouted questions reached inside the van, but the trespassers seemed to get the message that he was not going to stop.

Just as they pulled onto the street, a camera flashed. Beth emitted a startled cry. "Must they do that?"

"It's their job," Eden said, sounding more forgiving than she felt. She hated censorship in any form, but this kind of intrusion on a private family matter was plain bad manners—media insolence at its worst.

She glanced back at the house. The reporters were leaping into their cars and trucks. Her chest squeezed with impotent rage at their audacity. Beth didn't need this stress. Neither did she. Her gaze met David's in the rearview mirror, and she saw that he was aware of the media's intention of pursuing them.

Neither mentioned it to Beth, but Eden felt the van accelerate a notch and knew if it were at all possible, David would try to lose the unwanted company. That warm, fuzzy sensation tripped through her again, and Eden knew she must curtail it permanently; even if no one was bent on killing her, she was still the main suspect in a double murder, and David could not afford personally or professionally to be linked romantically with her. She would spare him that at all costs.

They left the housing development well ahead of the press cars and news trucks and, with a few trick turns, managed to reach I-90 without any sign of followers. Again her gaze met David's in the rearview mirror, and he winked at her. Immediately her body reacted, tingling sensuously in every intimate recess.

Damn the unfairness of life. She settled into the seat, unable to keep from staring at his wonderfully shaped head, from stealing glimpses of his incredible moss green eyes in the mirror.

"I really hate being a baby, Dr. Coulter," Beth said. "But I am scared."

"That's normal, Beth. But you'll be fine. In fact, soon you'll feel like a whole new you."

Beth was quiet a moment, as if contemplating the possibility that her life could ever take on any semblance of its old vitality. But Eden knew she'd dreamed of this constantly since they'd learned her kidneys were diseased.

Would any of their lives ever be normal again?

The old helplessness attacked Eden. She'd gladly have relinquished a kidney for Beth, but after initial testing, Beth had become sensitized to Eden's blood, rendering her ineligible as a donor.

Beth intruded on Eden's dismal musings, her voice laced with an optimistic lilt that hadn't been there for entirely too long. "Do you realize I might even be able to return to your class next winter?"

So much had occurred in the past year, Eden had all but forgotten how much Beth had enjoyed David's psych classes. She leaned forward and patted her on the shoulder. "God willing, sweetie, you'll be able to pick up all your classes."

"Here, here," David cheered.

For the third time, Eden's gaze met his in the mirror. She forced herself to look away. The early-evening traffic was light on the floating bridge, and the lowering sun reflected on the waters of Lake Washington like long, glittering Fourth of July sparklers as they drove toward Seattle and the university district.

They arrived unaccosted at the University of Washington Medical Center's Emergency entrance. Inside, few patients occupied the waiting area, and those who did cast the newest arrivals cursory glances, then lost interest. Still, Eden braced herself, knowing one person's recognizing her could change that.

The nurse at the admittance desk was round and jolly, her straw-colored hair pulled to the top of her head like a clown's cap. She greeted Beth as if she were expected and began recording check-in information. Only once did Eden suffer an uncomfortable moment, when the nurse glanced sideways at her as if trying to place where she knew her from. Beth noticed and frowned.

"Well, Ms. Montgomery, that's all *I* need from you." Setting the chart aside, the plump nurse lumbered out of her chair. "Soon as we get you in a hospital gown, this dog and pony show can begin."

Beth gripped Eden's hand.

"Will it be all right if I come, too?" Eden asked.

"It's fine with me." The nurse looked at Beth.

Beth pulled Eden aside and spoke in a lowered voice. "You know a slew of doctors will be in to see me. Are you sure you're up to facing them?"

Less than an hour ago, she'd have said a resounding no. But at this crucial moment, she realized it mattered very little what other people thought of her. "I'd face a tribe of starving cannibals for you."

"I appreciate that, Eden, but they're just running a bunch more tests. I can handle that on my own."

David stepped between them. "Eden, why don't you let me buy you a *latte?* I know I could use a jolt of caffeine."

"Yes, go," Beth said. "Then I won't worry about you."

That Beth should have to worry about anyone but herself at this time settled the matter. "Sure, sweetie. But if you change your mind, I'll be right out here." She gestured toward the waiting area, which was gaining new occupants with each passing minute.

Beth noticed the growing crowd, too, and frowned. "Just meet me upstairs later, okay?"

"Count on it." Eden kissed her sister's cheek, then spun around and fell into step with David. "Why do I suddenly feel like she's the older sister?"

"The loss of her physical strength has reduced her to a child in many ways this past year, but underneath she's the same, extremely mature twenty-three-year-old." David wanted to fold Eden's hand into his, but they didn't have the corridor to themselves and Beth's emergency hadn't changed the danger of their being seen together. Even this was risky. Still, they couldn't very well sneak around the hospital without looking absurd and guilty.

The fragrant aroma of espresso wafted through the third-floor entrance area. David approached the espresso bar while Eden selected a table in a secluded corner of the solarium, sat and plopped her purse on the floor. She watched David as he ordered *lattes,* and noticed two women walk past him and glance back. It struck her anew what a handsome man he was. Head-turningly so. The great thing was, he didn't seem to know it.

From out of nowhere, a shiver climbed her spine, an eerie, indefinable creepiness as if someone's gaze were drilling her back. Her neck prickled. She jerked her head up and glanced around, but the few couples huddled at neighboring tables seemed lost in conversation, and those people who were alone were either reading or enjoying the view out the garden sun windows.

No one was looking at her.

Paranoid. Stressed. Anxious for Beth. Any one or all three could explain the weird feeling. No one was watching her. She had to relax. She propped her elbows on the table and twined her fingers together. The sensation skittered over her again. Damn. Paranoid or not, she couldn't stay here.

As David started toward her, she crossed to him and accepted one of the *lattes*. "Is there someplace more private we could enjoy this?"

"Why?"

"Oh, nothing."

He studied her. "No, something. What?"

She shrugged. "I just felt as if someone was watching me. Silly, huh?"

"Maybe not." He scanned the area behind her and up and down the wide hallway. "I don't see anyone I recognize."

"It's probably my discomfort at being in public."

"Then let's go to my office. It will be a while before Beth is taken upstairs, and I should check my mail and phone messages."

THEY'D BEEN in his office ten minutes when the outer door opened.

"Probably housekeeping." David left Eden sitting beside his desk and went to investigate. "Lynzy. What are you doing here so late?"

Lynzy gave him a big grin. She wore a short black skirt and a midriff top. Her long brown hair swung loose around her shoulders. "I forgot my sunglasses." She retrieved them from her desk, then seemed to notice the open office door. "I didn't interrupt a session, did I?"

"No."

Recognizing the voice, Eden rose and walked toward them.

"Mrs. Prescott." There was no hesitancy in Lynzy's grin. "I heard on the radio that you'd been released. Congratulations."

"Thank you." Eden breathed a little easier.

Lynzy waved the hand holding the sunglasses in a gesture of dismissal. "I never believed all those horrid stories about you. Person's innocent till *proven* otherwise, I say. But if I were you, I'd be out celebrating, not here." Her dark eyebrows dipped low in a frown. "You aren't sick or anything?"

"Beth is down in the transplant wing," David answered. "Might have a kidney for her."

"Hooray." Impossibly Lynzy's face became more animated. "I'll keep my fingers crossed. Well, I'd better get home. I've got a dinner date." She started for the door, then spun around. "Oh, Doc, I passed Colleen on my way in. She said she's been trying to reach you on your cell phone."

"It's in my car, which, I'm afraid, is at the Prescotts'. I haven't listened to my voice mail yet, either. Do you know what Colleen wanted?"

"Apparently she left some letters on your desk that need signing."

"I've seen them."

"And to know about your schedule for tomorrow."

"If Beth has surgery, I'll probably be here until she's out of recovery. Kenneth Levy will cover my classes, and I've left Colleen a note to reschedule patients."

Lynzy shrugged. "Looks like you've thought of everything."

When Lynzy left, her energy seemed to desert the room with her, leaving Eden spent. "I wish I had her stamina."

David noticed how worn-out she looked. "It's been a long day. Come and sit down while I check my voice mail."

He led her back into his private office. As he reached for his telephone, Eden gladly sank into the thick leather chair across from his desk. Her eyelids felt heavy, as if she could close them for a week. She was too young to be this bone tired. Maybe a week in her own bed . . .

The thought broke off as she realized she could no more spend another week in that house than she could willingly go back to jail. Maybe it was time she told David about her suspicions concerning Valerie. She needed his opinion.

The moment he hung up the telephone, she said, "There's something I want to discuss with you."

"About Beth?"

"This is about my sister-in-law, your former patient. I know you can't divulge the root of her problems—why she was seeing you professionally—but I suspect it had something to do with Peter. You don't have to say yes or no, just hear me out."

She explained the conclusions she'd reached. He listened thoughtfully. It was one of those things she adored about him, that wonderful ability to really listen; his job notwithstanding, few people learned that talent. "Do you think Valerie is obsessed with you?" she concluded.

He looked bemused. "As is usual with a lot of patients, I'd say Valerie suffered some transference dependency, but she'd worked it out by the end of our sessions.''

''Are you certain?''

The question blindsided him, rousing his self-doubts. He had thought he'd read Rose Hatcher correctly and missed by miles. Could he be wrong about Valerie? Dare he dismiss Eden's suspicions out of hand? He considered for a long moment, then made up his mind. ''Maybe we should suspect everyone.''

''Maybe we should start compiling a list.''

''Yeah.'' David liked the idea. He'd been floundering for some course of action that might actually lead to unmasking the real killer. ''Colleen has paper and pencils in her desk.''

''I've got a tablet and a pen in my purse.'' Eden reached beside the chair for her purse but came away with a handful of air. She leaned over and scanned the floor on all sides of the chair and around the desk. ''David, I can't find my purse.''

''Did you leave it in the van?''

She considered. ''No, I had it in Emergency. I took out my insurance card to show the nurse when Beth was admitted.''

''Where else were we?''

It hit them at the same time. ''The solarium.''

''Oh, dear. I remember now. I set it down beneath the table while I waited for you. Then I had that weird feeling of being watched and I forgot all about it.''

They hurried back to the third floor. As they approached the solarium, Eden caught sight of a small swatch of tanned leather. ''It's still there. Shoved against the wall now.''

She grabbed the purse and, with her heart thumping, wrenched the clasp open. One look inside chilled her to the bone. Everything seemed in the same neat order she'd left it, with one exception: on top of her wallet lay a single white rose.

She let out a rush of air and dropped the purse as if it contained a huge spider.

David picked it up gingerly between his fingers. Spotting the rose, he swore. "Who the hell could have done this?"

"Whoever was watching me earlier."

Fear stole through David. Something dark and evil lurked within this place that represented life and hope. "The police—"

"Forget it. You said Kollecki didn't believe the roses meant anything. This won't change his mind. Besides, the hospital is out of his jurisdiction." Her mind raced. "You realize this blows my theory on Val."

"Not necessarily. We don't know that she's home."

"Good point." She caught his arm and dragged him to the nearest bank of pay phones. "There's one way of proving it."

A minute and a half later, Eden had dialed and was listening to the phone ring and ring. She pressed her lips together and started to replace the receiver. Valerie's voice resounded from the earpiece. "Hello! Hello?"

Eden didn't speak. She hung up and turned to David. "She answered."

"The first one on our list and the first one off. Don't look so disappointed. We'll find others and start a new list." He ached to hold her. With an effort, he curbed the urge and, settling for her elbow, guided her toward an elevator. "Beth ought to be upstairs. She'll be wondering if we've forgotten her."

They emerged on the fourth floor and started down the hall. Eden stopped dead in her tracks. David pulled up short, too. She couldn't believe her eyes. In the designated waiting area outside the transplant wing, two women reposed on the decorative chairs situated near the ladies' room.

One of the women was Valerie. Apparently she was having her calls forwarded to her cell phone.

David leaned toward Eden and whispered, "The list lives."

She nodded and strode to her sister-in-law's side. Valerie stood, wringing her hankie in her fingers. Eden kept her voice level. "Val, I told you I'd call as soon as we knew something."

"Ariel said she might be needed here."

Eden glanced at the woman beside Val. It was not Ariel Bell. "That doesn't explain why *you're* here."

Valerie drew in a noisy breath, and her voice took on a plaintive tone. "I couldn't stand waiting alone, so I came with her. Beth has been in my care these past weeks, you know, and I'm just as concerned for her welfare as you are."

The tiny declaration rang with sincerity, shaking Eden's confidence in Valerie's guilt. Admittedly Val had always treated Beth decently and with concern ever since she'd fallen ill. Was the thought of perhaps losing Beth so soon after losing Peter tearing Val up inside? Or was this just a clever performance by a cold-blooded murderer?

Eden felt the woman next to Val staring at her and, when she glanced at her again, her stomach dipped to her toes. She knew this face from the local six-o'clock news.

The woman stood and thrust a microphone she'd held out of view beneath her full skirt toward Eden. "Mrs. Prescott, perhaps you'd give me an exclusive?"

"Go away." David stepped in front of Eden. "Or I'll call security and have you escorted out."

A scruffy-looking female stepped from the ladies' room hefting a news camera on one shoulder, the lens scanning Eden and David. Eden turned back to Valerie. "How did they know to come here?"

"I guess they followed Ariel and me."

As if she hadn't heard David, the reporter continued. "Eden, Ms. Prescott generously shared the good news about the kidney donor for your sister. It's been quite a day for you. Won't you tell our watchers how you're coping?"

Eden tamped down her anger at Valerie, lifted her chin, squared her shoulders and said into the camera, "No comment."

She skirted the reporter and moved into the transplant wing. David escorted her to the nurses' station, found out which room Beth occupied and received two isolation masks. Handing one to Eden, he said, "Room's halfway down."

As they approached, two doors on opposite sides of the hall opened at the same time and a nurse wearing a mask emerged from each room. The first slipped hers off. It was Ariel Bell, whom Eden would have recognized regardless, thanks to her hot-pink pants uniform.

The second nurse stopped Ariel, and as they started chatting, removed her own mask. Eden's pulse wobbled. The second nurse was Denise Smalley.

Ariel turned and greeted them. Denise smiled at David, then glared at Eden. "Well, isn't this my lucky day?"

Eden let the sarcasm roll over her. "Ariel probably told you my sister has been admitted for her transplant."

"So has my patient—the backup recipient."

Eden knew a backup recipient was always notified in case the final cross-matching showed that the primary recipient, in this case Beth, had any preformed immunity to the donor, which would make her ineligible for the donated kidney.

But it was unnecessarily cruel of Denise to remind her. An intended spite. Eden restrained the urge to lash back at her. Since she'd been a small child, her mother had always told her the best wars were the ones walked away from with your dignity intact. "Don't cast the first stone, do defend your convictions and always be a lady," her mother had always said.

"Ariel, how is Beth doing?" Eden asked, ignoring the scathing look Denise cast her, but not missing the longing glance she sent David.

Ariel ran her hands through her unkempt hairdo, mussing it worse than usual, which perversely enhanced her adorable face. Her gaze shifted between David and Eden. "She's optimistic. But I think she'll be glad to see you."

David and Eden donned their masks and entered the room.

Beth was stretched out on the bed, her eyes closed. She had undergone a second set of testing, seen a second round of doctors and showered with a special antiseptic soap. Now she had to wait for the final cross-match. Once the call came that she was going for the transplant, antibiotics would be given intravenously just before she left for the operating room.

She opened her eyes. "Hi."

"How are you feeling?"

"I hate this waiting."

"Waiting is always the hardest part," David assured her. "But today has been a day of miracles for the Montgomery sisters. Eden's out of jail, and you're going to get your new kidney."

Eden said a silent prayer that he was right, that this donor would be the one who saved her sister's life. She added another prayer for people who marked their driver's licenses to be a donor, one for the miracle of modern medicine and one last prayer for the family whose loved one had lost his or her life.

Beth closed her eyes again.

Eden led David over to the window. The night pressed down against the glass, as dark as her thoughts. "Did you notice the way Denise Smalley looked at you?"

"Not really."

"Well, you should have. I think she has some kind of major crush on you."

David grinned. "No way."

Eden nodded. "I think we should add her to the list."

"But Shannon was her sister."

"Valerie being Peter's sister hasn't exempted her from suspicion."

He sighed. "Point taken."

"At least consider it. She and Shannon might have hated each other. And we should find out how long she's been on duty tonight. Maybe she was the one who put the rose into my purse."

"Okay. I'll meander down to the nurses' station and strike up a conversation with her." Above the mask, his green eyes shone with mischief. "See what kind of detective I am."

Eden smiled. "Be discreet, Sherlock."

"Certainly, my dear Watson." David left Eden sitting beside Beth's bed.

But Denise was not at the nurses' station. Valerie lurched out of the chair beside Ariel and rushed to him, making him wonder if Eden's prediction that Val still had tender feelings for him held some validity.

"How's Beth doing?" Valerie asked.

"I'm sure Ariel told you." He was not happy to see the reporter still hanging around and wasn't about to divulge information on Beth's condition to the press. He hoped Valerie started using some discretion in that area.

The news reporter was on him in a wink. "Dr. Coulter, could you spare me a moment?"

He waved her off. "As I stated earlier, I have nothing to say."

"Not even about Rose Hatcher's escape from prison?"

Chapter Seven

"Escaped?" David felt a shock jolt through his body with the force of a lightning bolt. "When?"

The reporter blinked at his raised voice. "About a month and a half ago."

"A month and a... That's not possible. If there'd been an escape from Purdy, every news network west of the Cascades would have covered the story."

Visibly regaining her practiced composure, the reporter spoke into her microphone. "Rose Hatcher didn't escape from Purdy. Apparently she caused some trouble up there in March and again in April, and they contracted with Oregon Women's Correctional Center in Salem to take her."

She shifted the microphone under his nose.

David growled, "How long have you known about this?"

"It was brought to my attention last week."

He blanched, suspecting his face was as white as the collar of the reporter's blouse. She frowned at him. "I've also heard rumors that she was recanting her confession. What do you think? *Did* she kill Marianne DePaul?"

"I—I have no thoughts about that." But he did. God help him, he did. Hanging on to what little remained of his composure, he wheeled around and headed back down the hall to Beth's room, but he stayed outside. He needed to catch his breath, to sort out what it all meant.

He leaned against the wall, disbelief and shock tumbling inside him. Rose Hatcher had been on the loose since before Peter and Shannon were murdered. He didn't know whether to be relieved for Eden's sake or terrified for all their sakes. Did Kollecki know about this? He must. Must have known for weeks. Damn his ornery hide.

Anger chased the chill from his blood and slowed his ragged breathing. David shoved away from the wall, opened the door and stepped into Beth's room. Dr. Ingalls was there, a tall, rangy man with thick, wavy brown hair, who bore a striking resemblance to Elliott Gould.

He acknowledged David with a somber nod, then turned back to his patient. "I'm sorry, Beth. The crossmatching has ruled you ineligible for the available kidney."

A breath shuddered from Beth, shaking her thin body, and her shoulders slumped as if the doctor's words had stolen the very life from her. The silence that followed was painful, then Beth lifted her head and tried giving Eden a brave smile. It wobbled and died.

Helplessness descended on David like a slab of lead, robbing him of words and actions; he wanted to go to Beth but couldn't move. Not even when tears streamed unchecked down her face. She emitted a cry of frustration and yanked the IV tube from her arm.

Dr. Ingalls lurched forward, alarm widening his eyes. "Please, Beth, don't—"

"Leave me alone." Beth flung herself off the bed with a surprising strength she hadn't shown in months. She slammed open the closet, dragged her clothes off the hanger and began tugging off the hospital gown.

Eden rushed to assist her.

The hospital gown pooled at Beth's feet, but she showed no sign of caring that she stood naked before everyone.

David caught Dr. Ingalls by the arm. "Let's let them handle this." The two men left the room.

Beth hauled her sweatshirt over her head, tossing her bra at the overnight bag, oblivious that it snagged on one of the Velcro fasteners to dangle on the outside.

Eden said softly, "Hey, slow down, huh?"

"I can't. I can't."

Eden leaned over, retrieved and packed the bra. "I understand the frustration you're feeling, sweetie... and the fury... and the injustice."

Beth stopped at that. She stared long and hard at Eden, then nodded. She wiped her face on her sleeve, sniffled and exhaled loudly. "I just want to get out of here... as far away as possible."

"We can do that."

Beth's surge of energy subsided, and she accepted Eden's help getting into her sweatpants and loafers. Eden hoisted the overnight bag and offered Beth her free arm for support. As they reached the door, Beth said, "Oh, don't forget your purse."

Eden glanced at the offending object perched in the visitor's chair, and her throat constricted. At least Beth had taken her mind off of the rose... for a while. But as she gathered her purse to her side, a delicate scent lifted from its depths, tickling the air with a noxious stench reminiscent of funereal flowers.

David waited in the hall for them. An ashen hue tinged his complexion as though he were somehow more upset about this than even Beth. How could that be? Granted, he was a caring doctor, but he wasn't the one whose life hinged on a donor kidney, and although he knew Beth's condition worsened daily, he believed in the power of positive thinking.

Yet he had not offered one encouraging maxim. Anxiety roiled through Eden's empty stomach. Something was terribly amiss. Had he perhaps discovered Denise Smalley might be a candidate for their suspect list?

The walk to the waiting area felt as short as a walk off a gangplank into a sea of uncertainty, and gazing ahead, Eden saw the waters were full of predators. Both Valerie and Ariel wore concerned expressions and converged on Beth like a pair of curious crabs plucking at her with their verbal claws.

Valerie reached for Beth, then stayed her hand. "David told us the bad news." Her voice was weepy. "Now, don't you worry, dear. They'll find another donor real soon."

Eden wanted to tell Valerie to put a sock in it, but she noticed the reporter and her camera person circling nearby.

Ariel gave Beth a huge smile and snagged the hem of her sweatshirt in her thin fingers, straightening it. "Ah, you'll feel better when you're home in your own bed."

From the corner of her eye, Eden saw the reporter was menacingly close now, the camera riding her companion's shoulder like a black dorsal fin. Eden tensed, feeling as though she were about to be devoured by the great white media.

The reporter spoke into her microphone. "Mrs. Prescott, er, Eden. We've heard the bad news. How do you feel?" She shifted toward Beth. "How do *you* feel, Ms. Montgomery?"

As the microphone snaked toward her, Beth wrenched free of Eden.

"No." Panic filled her eyes, and she lunged at David, grabbing his shirtfront and burying her head against his chest. Like a sick child, she bawled, "Keep her away from me. Keep her away from me. Keep her away."

David roared at the newswomen, "Back off!"

"Could you people please lower your voices?" Denise Smalley's anger had her face scrunched like an overripe prune. "This is not a war zone."

She glared at the reporter and camerawoman. "I believe Dr. Coulter asked you to leave. Let me second that."

The camera kept rolling. The reporter kept speaking into her mike.

"Today a judge claimed Eden Prescott's Fourth Amendment rights were violated in the procurement of the weapon used to murder her husband and his fiancée. She was released from prison—all charges dropped. In a rare irony of events tonight, the sister of Shannon Smalley, Denise Smalley, actually defended Mrs. Prescott against questioning by this reporter." She shoved the microphone at Denise. "Would you like to say anything about that, Ms. Smalley?"

"I never..." Denise's face was crimson. She poked a finger at the reporter. "That does it. I'm calling security."

"Don't bother. We've got enough. We're leaving." The newswomen moved off and boarded an elevator.

Valerie turned on Eden, her face red with fury, her eyes wild with hate. "If you hadn't tricked the police into setting you free, the rest of us wouldn't have been subjected to this media persecution."

Eden clamped her mouth shut, too angry to trust what she might do or say.

Ariel shook her head, her straw-colored hair shifting like wind through a haystack. "Could we please get my patient home?"

Beth's eyes flew wide at the suggestion. "No. I can't go back to that house. There will just be more reporters there."

Eden gently stroked Beth's back. "We aren't going back to that house, sweetie, not ever."

"What?" Valerie stiffened as if Eden had struck her. "What do you mean, never coming back? I don't pretend to like it, Eden, but you do own half of the house."

"Then you can buy my share from me, Val. Or you can sell it and give me half of the proceeds. But I won't live under the same roof with a woman who thinks I murdered her brother." *A woman I think might be the real murderer.*

Valerie stepped back, her face crimson. But she didn't bother to deny the accusation. She turned to Ariel. "I'm ready to leave now."

As Val stalked to the elevators, Ariel glanced at Eden. "Are you terminating me?"

"Oh, no, Ariel." She softened her expression. "But I'm not sure yet where we'll be. May I call you tomorrow?"

"Of course. If I'm not at my apartment, leave a message."

David, Beth and Eden waited until they were gone, then withdrew to his office. Beth collapsed on the sofa and was soon asleep.

Night draped the windows. David and Eden stood beside his desk. Inches separated them. He studied her face, detecting the pain and disappointment of the past few hours. He ached to comfort her, but the need heating his blood restrained him; he didn't trust himself to offer her only comfort, and right now her needs were more important than his. He tore the top page from his desk calendar. "Have you decided where you're going yet?"

She let out a weary sigh. "No."

He swallowed hard. "I have two guest rooms."

Her gaze met his. Was it only a few hours ago that he'd demanded she stay away from him? Now he was offering to open his home to her and her sister. She loved him for it. His house held a lot of warm memories for her; however, right now it was the second-to-last place she would feel safe. "Don't you think the reporters would figure that out soon enough?"

He frowned, and that odd glint she'd noticed in his eyes earlier reappeared. Uneasiness danced over her skin. What had happened to cause that glint? Before she could ask, he snapped his fingers. "I have an idea. Let me make a call."

He went into the outer office and used Colleen's phone. Eden settled her weary body into the leather chair facing his desk. She strained to hear his end of the conversation, picking up the sound of his voice but not what he was saying. She shut her eyes, opening them minutes later when she felt his presence. He stood over her, his gaze filled with tenderness. Her heart quickened.

"I just talked my brother, James, into lending us a rental house he has vacant at the moment. It's on Lake Retreat, a beautiful old Victorian with a fence on both sides of the property and a lawn that slopes down to the lake. It even has a private dock and a rowboat."

A rowboat? He'd said it as if he were a Realtor intent on selling her the place. Despite the seriousness of the situation, she grinned.

He rounded his desk, dropped into the chair and scrawled something on a notepad. "James is meeting us out back in twenty minutes. We're going to exchange your van for his car."

Her grin faltered, and she eyed him incredulously. "Why the extra precaution—surely not because someone left a rose in my *abandoned* purse?"

David tensed and glanced away from her as though he couldn't stand her scrutiny. He vacated his chair in a jerky movement and strode to the window, yanking the miniblind cord and staring out into the street below. Eden stepped up behind him. He glanced over his shoulder at her.

She ached to touch him, to smooth away the twin frown lines between his eyebrows. She curled her fingers against her palm. "What's going on?"

A sigh slipped from his lips, and he spun away from the window. But before he could answer, Beth yawned loudly, grabbing their attention. She pulled herself into a sitting position. "Sorry, I guess I drifted off."

Beth knew nothing of the stalker, and Eden preferred keeping it that way. She walked to the sofa and sat down beside her. "It's all right, sweetie, you needed the sleep."

"Have you figured out where we're going?"

"Yep. David has taken care of that."

As he repeated his description of the lake house, Eden gazed at his beloved face. What had him so edgy? She knew they were still in danger, but this felt so very immediate. It had to be more than the rose. What? Sometime before this night ended, he and she were going to have a long talk.

Beth had a dozen questions about the house and the lake. David answered each one patiently, then glanced at his watch. "Come on, you two. Gather your belongings. James will be cooling his heels in the parking lot by now."

Cooling seemed the operative word. The night air stole through Eden's silk pantsuit with gelid fingers, embracing her, lifting goose bumps. In all the excitement over Beth, she had neglected bringing a coat but she hadn't missed having one—until now.

The only comfort was that no reporters lurked in this parking lot. She'd bet the same couldn't be said for the parking lot where her van waited.

She hugged herself against the chill as David introduced them to his older brother. James Coulter was a handsome, fortyish Seattle businessman who looked as if he'd be more at home in a three-piece business suit than in the Levi's and sweater he wore now. He was heavier than David by at least thirty pounds, and gray streaked his brown hair at the temples.

David insisted Beth and she get into the car while James and he finished talking.

"Everything you asked for is in the trunk. The keys to the house are on the ring here." James handed the keys of his year-old Cadillac Seville to David. "The insurance is paid, but don't make me collect on it...if you can help it."

David laughed. He gave James instructions on where to find Eden's van and climbed behind the wheel. Beth sat in back, nodding off again.

As exhausted as she was, Eden sat rigidly on the front passenger seat beside David. The motor purred, and the luxury of the car enfolded her like nothing had done in ages. She drew in a deep, tired breath. The smell of rich leather invaded her nose and her senses, thankfully eradicating the cloying, hated scent of the rose.

But not the danger it evoked.

She gazed out at the lighted street, but the tinted car windows enhanced the ominous feel of the night. Who had watched her at the solarium? Was she watching still?

As they left the university district and got on I-5, Eden saw David constantly checking the rearview mirror. Was *she* following them even now? The thought strangled her. Maybe there was no safe place to hide.

Traffic on the I-90 floating bridge was modest. David alternated between driving the speed limit and ten miles per hour under it, keeping alert for anyone who mirrored his actions. Afraid Beth might overhear, Eden clutched her hands in anxious silence, wrestling the physical ache to ask if he saw anyone or anything suspicious.

Thirty minutes passed with the speed of three hours. He exited the freeway at Issaquah, drew to a stop at the red light and glanced her way. She could see him clearly beneath the streetlight. He sent her a reassuring grin and gently shook his head. She drew a wobbly breath and swallowed over the lump in her throat. They took the Issaquah-Hobart road out of town, proceeded past the access onto Highway 18, continued on through the town of Hobart and finally stopped at the light in Ravensdale.

"Just a few more miles," David said, turning east.

Minutes later they were on Lake Retreat Drive, a narrow, tree-lined road following the shoreline of Lake Retreat. Residences, impossible to define in the dark with only the flash of the Cadillac's headlights sweeping over them, embraced the land between water and road.

David slowed, then stopped before a six-foot-tall, moss-stained wooden fence. Nothing advertised the property's availability for lease. "I thought you said the house was for rent."

"James leases it from September to the end of May. He keeps it available for his private use during the summer, so he and his family can get away from the city whenever the mood strikes." David got out, unlocked the gate, drove through and closed and secured it from inside.

Eden eyed the lofty pine trees huddled overhead, swaying and creaking in the gusty wind as if warning them to leave this private sanctuary. The Cadillac rolled onward, down the dirt driveway toward a huge black hulk that could only be the house.

A shiver skittered over Eden at its forbidding appearance. "It'll look better with lights on, right?"

"Definitely." David chuckled.

He parked the Cadillac at an angle, aiming the headlights at a door with an oval etched-glass window in its center. The charm of the entrance and the wraparound porch shattered Eden's misgivings. This would be all right after all.

"Stay here until I get the lights turned on." David scrambled out of the car, and minutes later they were all inside the house.

"Wow." Beth blinked, only half-awake, taking in the living room with its three sofas, single end table and twin floor lamps, the extent of its furnishings, all arranged around the Victorian fireplace. "It's big."

"And cold." Eden whirled in a circle, eyeing the naked windows and the bare oak floor. Her every footstep emitted an eerie reverberation.

"And it echoes." David's impression of Bela Lugosi was stereotypically perfect.

Beth laughed. Eden gazed her way and grinned. "Call me a party pooper, but what heats this place anyway?"

David crossed to a thermostat. "In a few hours, we'll be nice and toasty. Meanwhile I'll start a fire. We might want to sleep in here. There's a couch for everyone, and James provided sleeping bags and some food."

Eden helped him unload the car. They returned a moment later with laden arms. David dropped the sleeping bags in the living room, and Eden carried the grocery sacks into the kitchen, a large, charming room done in peach and mint green, with cream-colored tile counters. The appliances were modern and included a microwave and a Mr. Coffee; obviously James and family liked their comforts.

She pulled a coffee can from one of the sacks. An hour ago, she'd been ready to collapse. Now she doubted she could sleep. The coffee was just starting to drip when David came in.

"Finding everything all right?"

"As though I were at home." She noticed with some surprise that she no longer tensed at every sound.

"Coffee'll be ready soon, and I've got TV dinners in the microwave."

"Smells wonderful. I've got the fire started. Why don't you go sit with Beth and warm up? I'll bring in the food when it's ready."

For Beth's sake, they kept the conversation light while they ate. Like a child who had spent a long and tiring day, she nearly fell asleep over her fettucini and made no protests about climbing into her sleeping bag.

Eden cleared away the dirty food containers and refilled David's and her cups, then returned to the living room. He sat on the floor, his back propped against a sofa, his knees drawn to his flat stomach. Beth slept, her even breathing vying with the soft hiss of the burning logs. Eden settled beside him. Absently he took the cup she offered, but his gaze remained fixed on the fire, while a muscle in his jaw twitched to the rhythm of his thoughts.

Obviously, all-consuming thoughts.

Her patience snapped. "All right. What's going on? You've been worrying about something for hours now."

He tossed back a healthy swig of coffee, glancing at her only when he set the cup down again. "You'd better brace yourself."

He related his encounter with the TV reporter and the bombshell she'd dropped about Rose Hatcher.

The heat drained from Eden's cheeks. She scooted up and sat on the sofa, her gaze flying toward the window, seeing her own reflection flickering like a ghost in the cold panes. "Do you think she could have killed Peter and Shannon?"

"It makes sense. Shannon's was the second name on that hit list the cops found in Rose's apartment."

His words filled her ears and screamed through her mind like the shrill cry of a hungry hyena. Eden hugged herself. Neither the fire nor the coffee could touch the chill swirling inside her. There was no doubt in her mind that her name was now at the top of Rose Hatcher's list. No doubt that only a fluke had spared her from the deadly trap Rose had set for her.

But what new trap was Rose setting?

Chapter Eight

The fear on Eden's face shattered David's resolve to keep his distance. He scooted onto the sofa and took her hands into both of his own. She glanced at their entwined fingers, then up into his face. Tears shimmered in her beautiful eyes, wetting her thick lashes, but she jutted her chin as if willing them not to fall.

"I'll always be here for you, Eden. You don't have to be brave for me."

She grinned lopsidedly and gently squeezed his hand. "How easy it would be to collapse. God knows, I'm tired enough and frightened enough, but I won't surrender my life without a fight."

She glanced at Beth with the same tenderness and love in her eyes that she'd shown for him. "On a cold summer night very much like this one, when I was nineteen and living in an apartment with three other girls, and Beth was fourteen and attending a slumber party, our parents died. A house fire."

Her voice broke, and she lifted her chin a notch higher. "A neighbor managed to save Mom, but she was badly burned. For two excruciating weeks, she clung to life through unimaginable pain. Watching her struggle, I realized how precious life was to her, how precious it must always be to me. So you see, I do need to be brave. For myself. It's the only defense I have against Rose Hatcher.''

At first glance, he supposed most people took Eden for a fragile woman who'd quail at the very thought of personal hardship, but she proved correct the old adage about not judging a book by its cover. Petite, yes. Fragile, no. He admired that inner strength. He glanced at Beth. ''We're going to have to tell her.''

''I know.'' Eden leaned against him. If only this haven were the reality of their lives: a safe, normal environment where love could blossom. But it was as much a prison as the King County Jail—only here, the bars were tall pines, a lake and a moss-stained fence.

Suddenly she felt as if she couldn't breathe. She shoved up and off the sofa and stepped to the fireplace, her back to the uncovered window panes and whatever eyes might be peering in at them. David came up behind her, wrapped his arms around her and pulled her back against him. Eden closed her eyes, welcoming the warmth his body sent into hers, the strength.

Gently, like a couple dancing in place to a much-loved song only they could hear, she swayed with him, feeling her distress lifting, lifting as David was lifting her now, cradling her in his arms. She locked her hands behind his neck, lolled her head against his shoulder, her body snug to his chest.

Holding her like a child, he continued to sway, until Eden gave in to her exhaustion and fell asleep. David eased her down on the sofa, lowered her head to the pillow and pulled the sleeping bag to her chin. He ached to climb into that bag beside her and hold her all night. He settled for brushing his lips across her silken cheek.

Then he rechecked the door and window locks, tossed another log on the fire, doused the lights and hunkered into his own sleeping bag.

THE PUNGENCY of frying bacon and fresh-brewed coffee filtered into Eden's consciousness, clearing away the last vestiges of sleep. She inhaled deeply. To her dismay, the action sent a violent lurch through her stomach—the usually adored aromas inducing nausea. She stumbled from the sofa, hurried into the tiny bathroom off the foyer and retched.

A minute later, with her stomach empty if somewhat unsettled, she splashed cold water on her face and glanced at her reflection in the oak-framed oval mirror. Her complexion was the color of fresh snow. Her legs felt rubbery. Her eyes looked bruised. And she was so exhausted, she wanted to sleep forever. "Damn you, Rose Hatcher. Stalking my dreams. Haunting my life."

Her words to David about not giving up her life stilled her tirade. Falling apart was something Valerie would do. Not her. But how would she manage to pull herself together? If she were home, she'd start with a shower and clean clothes; feeling physically put together usually boosted her spirits.

Instead, she was stuck in this awful pantsuit that looked like a cousin to an accordion and hair that poked up where it ought to lie flat. She could do nothing for her clothes, but her hair was another matter. She sprinkled water on the offending tresses and finger-combed it into a semblance of its usual style, then pinched her cheeks.

Not much improvement, she decided, but the best she could manage at the moment.

She returned to the living room. Despite its lack of window covering, despite the sunny day, shadows dominated, creating a gloomy aura—thanks, Eden realized, to the trees that hugged the high side of the lot.

In total contrast, the kitchen was as bright as if it were a raft in the middle of the lake, and David as sunny as its assigned life guard. He was standing at the stove, juggling pots and pans whose contents reeked of stomach-churning aromas. She forced a smile. "Good morning."

He grinned at her. "Afternoon, actually."

Eden nodded. She could not look at the food. Smelling it was difficult enough. Her gaze rolled over the oak table to the picture window and the glorious view of sloping green lawn and lake. Beth's frail body and ebony hair caught her attention. She sat, hugging her knees, on a sturdy-looking dock watching a fisherman cast and reel.

Beside Beth, bobbing in the water, was the much-acclaimed rowboat, but Eden was instantly concerned about the fisherman not being who or what he seemed. "Should Beth be out there in full view of—?"

"Don't worry." David cut her off. The oven banged open. Eden glanced at him in time to see the platter resting on the oven shelf, a heap of bacon hugging one side, to which he was adding more slices. "This lot is completely private, from neighbors and passersby alike."

A beautiful prison, Eden thought, strolling to the table, noticing for the first time that it was set for three. Apricot-colored paper napkins nestled on the muted green stoneware plates. She stroked the top of one of the oak chairs. "I can't believe James rents this house furnished. Isn't he afraid someone will steal some of these antiques?''

''The same couple has rented it for five years. They have no children and travel all summer. It's a perfect situation for both parties.'' David placed a pitcher of orange juice on the table. ''It is a great old house, isn't it?''

Recalling the parallels she'd been drawing between this house and jail, she felt her cheeks heat. But the truth was, under other circumstances, she might appreciate the house's attributes, instead of dwelling on its negative aspects. ''I like this room, but the living room isn't as warm as I would have done it.''

He broke eggs into a bowl. ''Did you decorate your house?''

Picturing the formal decor at ''Prescott Manor,'' Eden laughed. ''Oooh, nooo. Peter insisted on hiring professionals. *His* house had to reflect his wealth and his exquisite good taste. His wealthy colleagues and clients were meant to envy him.''

David stirred the eggs, added milk and seasoning, stirred again, then poured them into a frying pan. ''How would you have decorated it?''

Considering the question, she strode to the toaster and plunked in two slices of bread. ''I'm not sure. But certainly in a way that exhibited something of the personalities of the people who lived there...the way your house does.''

His neck reddened at the compliment, at the thought it provoked of his partially furnished living room, and he wanted to drop the subject as he'd dropped his interest in that project when Marianne DePaul was murdered. His preoccupation with searching down the perfect furnishings had been the very thing distracting his attention from Rose Hatcher's obsession.

She glanced over her shoulder. He was dishing the scrambled eggs onto the platter in the oven. Her stomach rolled, and she drew a steadying breath. "How long have you owned your house?"

"Six years now. Our great-uncle Harry left James this house and me the one on Lake Washington." He lifted the platter toward her. Eden backed away.

David headed for the table. "Brunch is served. You'd better get yourself some coffee."

"I'm going to pass on the coffee. My stomach is protesting all the acid I've dumped into it lately." She pulled the bread from the toaster and added another two slices. "In fact, at the risk of offending you, I think I'd better stick to some dry toast."

"Maybe you're coming down with something." He placed the platter on a hot pad, then came to her and felt her forehead.

She chuckled, embarrassed, and brushed at his arm, but the contact disconcerted her. Their gazes locked, and she could see he wanted to pull her into his arms, to kiss her, and more. God help her, she wanted that, too. But they could not afford to get lost in passion with Beth so near.

With Rose Hatcher perhaps somewhere just as near.

Eden stacked the toast on the plate and carried it to the table, glancing out the window again. The lake was a cool sparkling green, much like David's eyes. She heard him scrape back a chair and sit. "I'll get Beth."

But Beth was already heading toward the house.

"She's on her way." David patted the spot to his right.

Keeping her eyes off the food, Eden joined him. A cellular phone was lying next to his place setting. She studied his face. "Have you called Kollecki?"

David scooped scrambled eggs onto his plate, then grabbed a bunch of bacon. "He didn't believe a stranger put the rose in your purse."

"Big surprise." Eden reached for a piece of dry toast.

"Hell, he's convinced—" With his eyes flashing angrily, David snatched up the pitcher and poured orange juice into three juice glasses, plunking the last in front of Eden, totally forgetting she was avoiding acid.

"You know what he's convinced of." David's neck was tinged red. "He hasn't warned anyone of Rose's escape. Said she was spotted in Southern California two days ago and will soon be back in custody. To which he added, 'She's not dumb enough to come back to Washington.' So I called Colleen and Lynzy and warned them myself."

Eden started. "Their names were on the list?"

He nodded. "In fact, Rose Hatcher was actually a friend of both Lynzy and Colleen."

"And me." Beth walked into the kitchen, her face pink either from exertion or too much sun.

But Eden was too preoccupied to worry about sunburn. She hadn't realized the class Beth had taken with David was the same class Rose and Marianne DePaul were in. "How well did you know Rose?"

"Fairly well." Beth sat down, spooned a small portion of eggs onto her plate and grabbed one piece of bacon from the stack. Instead of taking a bite, she shoved the food around with her fork. "Well enough to be shocked that she'd commit a violent act against someone. It seemed so...I don't know...out of character."

Eden glanced at David, wondering if he agreed with this assessment of Rose, but he seemed lost in some thought of his own. Was it about Rose, or something else? She glanced back at Beth. "Out of character— how?"

Beth's blue eyes rounded. "Well, she always struck me as one of those people who'd... oh, you know... *coax* a fly out of a room rather than swat it."

Eden took another bite of toast, hoping her stomach would settle down. "What was Marianne DePaul like?"

"I didn't care for her." Beth tried the eggs and grimaced. "She was such a suck-up."

David wasn't sure if his teaching ability had just been challenged or his cooking ability. He grinned. "I thought Marianne showed great promise."

"Yeah, and it went right to her head." Beth stopped her fork halfway to her mouth. "Say, why are we talking about Rose and Marianne?"

Eden had dreaded this moment. She'd also spent agonizing hours considering how to best broach the subject without terrifying Beth. She'd never thought Beth would provide the perfect opening. "There's something we need to discuss with you."

Brunch ended abruptly, appetites vanishing with the serious swing of the conversation.

Beth seemed to take the news with equal doses of shock and outrage and fear. She shoved her plate away, the pitiful portion of food she'd doled herself still clinging to it. "Lynzy and Colleen must be freaked."

"They'll take extra precautions and keep their eyes out for Rose." David stood, gathered dirty dishes and carried them to the sink.

Eden also felt the need for activity. She collected the remaining plates and brought them to the counter. David ran soapy water in the sink.

Beth's voice sliced through the tension invading the cheery kitchen. "Eden, what about my dialysis? I have an appointment in a couple of hours."

David shut off the water. "Not to worry. We'll get you there." At Eden's questioning glance, he added, "James will be here soon with your van."

Eden had a bad feeling about this, but she decided to keep it to herself.

"I wish I could shower and change my clothes," Beth muttered loudly enough for them to hear.

"I'll tell you what," David said, with a jovial lilt Eden doubted he felt. "While you're at dialysis, Eden and I'll stop by the house. Eden can pick up some clothes for you both and anything else you want."

Beth's raven eyebrows dipped in a frown. "But what if Rose is watching the house and follows you back here?"

Eden walked to the table and caught Beth's hand. "We'll be extra cautious."

"Eden," Beth said, "you don't even know what she looks like."

"David told me, but at any rate, you know."

Beth's eyebrow took a stubborn arch. "She has bright red hair that reaches to her waist, and she's petite, about your size."

"I'll keep my eyes peeled for her, but Detective Kollecki assures us that Rose is in California. So we're probably worrying about nothing."

Still, Beth frowned. "What about the reporters?"

David and Eden exchanged glances, then he reached for the cell phone and dialed. Eden shrugged and shook her head at Beth; she had no idea who he was calling.

David said, "Valerie, it's me. Yes, Beth is fine. I swear." He blew out an exasperated breath, and Eden sat down beside Beth, pitying David the tirade obviously pouring from her sister-in-law. His eyes narrowed in frustration. "Valerie, are the reporters still hanging around the house?"

There was a pause. Then he said, "Go look. Now." While he waited, he rolled his eyes to the ceiling, then gazed at Eden. "She claims she told the reporters you were never coming back and they actually believed her and left. But I'm having her double-check."

Before Eden could respond, he spoke again into the receiver. "Yes, Valerie, I'm still here. Thank you." Another pause. "Just curious, that's all. Goodbye."

He hung up and explained, "She wanted to know why I was asking about the reporters. I figured it was better to let her speculate. No telling what she'd do if she knew we would be showing up there later."

The reporters were actually gone. The tension in Eden's stomach eased, and she felt the first stirring of confidence that the toast would stay put.

"What about Ariel?" Beth asked.

"Oh, dear," Eden said. "I'd forgotten her."

Eden explained her decision to Beth, then used the phone. It was answered on the fifth ring. "Ariel, it's Eden Prescott."

The nurse greeted her warmly, then promptly asked about her patient. Eden assured her that Beth was well.

"Good." Ariel sounded relieved. "I've worried all morning whether or not anyone remembered she had dialysis today, but I had no way to contact you."

"She remembered."

"Would you like me to come and take her?"

"Er, no. I'll be able to take care of Beth by myself for the immediate future, so I'm afraid we won't be needing your services for the time being."

There was a long pause, and Eden could swear she felt a cool wind whistle down the line.

Then Ariel said, "I see." Not one speck of warmth remained in her voice. "I take it you've found a place to stay?"

"Yes. I'll be leaving you a check—which will include two weeks' severance—at Valerie's this afternoon. You can pick it up anytime after four today."

"Thank you. That's very generous. I'll call Ms. Prescott this evening, then." Her tone was a scant two degrees less chilly. "Tell Beth my thoughts are with her."

Later, luck was with them. Not one reporter lurked near the Prescott house. The only problem Eden faced was convincing David that she could handle packing her and Beth's suitcases without a bodyguard. "You have to collect your own clothes, plus you have patients to check on. It will save hours of time if we do these things separately, and we can get back to the lake house before dark."

"I don't know, Eden." He stared out at the house. "Valerie—"

"Valerie's less of a worry now. I'm not afraid of her now that Rose Hatcher is on the loose and the more likely suspect. And I'll be extra cautious about being followed."

He didn't like it, but her chin was set as hard as concrete, and if that weren't enough, David knew she would resent his dogging her like a police guard, treating her as if she couldn't take care of herself. He tucked the cellular phone into her hand. "I've got another in my car. If anything odd occurs—anything—call."

He waited until the front door of the house swung open before driving away.

"EDEN?" Valerie's ginger eyebrows shot up in surprise, but a smirk brought them back in a flash. "I knew you'd change your mind about moving out. Where's Beth?"

"Dialysis. And I haven't changed my mind, Val. I'm here for our clothes." Eden swept through the door and hurried to her room.

"For your clothes?" Valerie had arrived on her heels, out of breath and huffing like a disgruntled steam engine. She hovered in the doorway. "I can't believe you're actually doing this to me."

And why not? Eden wondered. Valerie was willing to believe worse of her. Eden spread her Luis Vuitton luggage, last year's Christmas gift from Peter, on the bed. "It was inevitable, Val. You need to accept that and decide what you want to do about the house."

"Well, I..." She humphed, clamped her mouth shut and stomped off.

Five minutes later, as Eden piled clothes and toilet articles into the various bags, she glimpsed Valerie once again standing in the doorway. She gave an exasperated sigh. "What's the matter, Val? Worried I'll take something that belongs to you?"

"No telling what you're capable of."

"May I remind you that everything in this room belongs to me."

"Not Peter's things."

"You know what? You're more than welcome to any and all of Peter's belongings."

"That's—that's very generous of you." For the second time, Valerie left her alone.

Eden finished packing her clothes, loaded her suitcases into the van, then started on Beth's room. Oddly she felt a little light-headed. Probably lifting all the bags with only a single slice of toast for energy. She shook her head, trying to shake off the sensation. It threw her off balance.

She sat on the bed and emptied Beth's underwear into a suitcase. Then, drawing a steadying breath, she crossed the room to tackle the closet. Without warning, the room lurched, and a pit like a black hole seemed to open at her feet and drag her down.

From some dark well, Eden swore she heard the high screech of a bird calling her name. She opened her eyes in a squint.

Valerie knelt beside her, a wild expression on her face. "My God, you scared me half to death. I came in here to see if I could help and found you facedown on the floor."

Eden struggled to a sitting position. Had she fainted? She must have.

Valerie's face was mottled. "Aren't you eating?"

"Of course I'm eating."

"Well, people don't faint without reason. You should see a doctor."

Using the bed for support, Eden hoisted herself to her feet. "Why do you care, Val? You think I murdered Peter."

"I don't care." Valerie backed away. "It's no skin off my nose."

"Good, because I'm fine." She was fine. Great, in fact. So she'd fainted. It meant nothing—nothing important anyway. She was just weak from lack of sleep and too much stress.

"Nevertheless, you did faint." Valerie crossed to the closet and gathered Beth's clothes as if they were a fat child she was hugging and carried them to the bed. When Eden had finished the packing, Valerie insisted on helping carry the remaining luggage to the van.

Eden reached for the last bag. Valerie was glancing at the road, frowning. "What's she doing here?"

"Who?" Eden jerked her head toward the street. A black compact was rolling to a stop at the corner, too far away now for her to see more than the red shine of its taillights.

Valerie's frown deepened, but she lifted her head haughtily. "I thought that was—" She bit off the words and shoved the last bag at Eden, the expression in her eyes unfriendly. "Never mind. It wouldn't be the first time I've been mistaken about something . . . or someone."

Eden sighed. "I'll talk to you later, Val."

Valerie headed back into the house, and Eden was grateful to be alone again. She drove to Redmond, still feeling weak.

Maybe she should see a doctor. She had to admit she hadn't felt especially well lately, but surely nothing much was wrong. Then why had she fainted? A niggling voice inside her head began adding disturbing symptoms together, and suddenly Eden realized something might actually be very wrong.

With time to spare before picking Beth up, she pulled into the parking lot of a strip mall and entered a drugstore. She was probably wrong, but there was an easy way to find out. Feeling self-conscious, she located the right aisle and perused the shelves, quickly spotting the item she sought. She grasped the package and began reading the back of the box.

Inexplicably a shiver crept down her spine, the same eerie tingling she'd had in the hospital solarium...as though someone was once again spying on her. She cast a sharp glance around. Two rows in front of her, she caught sight of carrot red hair behind the shelves.

She stuffed the box she'd been holding onto the shelf in front of her, logo side forward, then hurried to where she'd seen the redhead. The red hair belonged to a clerk stocking shelves—a woman tall enough to be seen over the top shelf. Rose Hatcher was supposedly petite. *Like her.*

Eden grinned at herself. So she was a lousy detective.

She returned to the aisle she'd occupied earlier, to the box she'd been reading. Her mouth went dry. It was back side out. She'd left it the other way around. Apprehension grabbed her. This time she scanned the store in all directions.

But no one seemed to be watching her or in a hurry to depart, and worse, no one looked vaguely familiar.

Willing herself to calm down, she reached for the box, but the oddest sensation that her nemesis had just handled it made her select the one beside it.

The self-conscious feeling she'd had entering the store doubled as she waited in line to purchase the item; she imagined the other customers' disapproving eyes, their knowing smirks. And the clerk offered no relief, moving with the speed of a snail, then taking forever to find the brown bag she requested for the package.

She crossed the parking lot, mumbling about the convenience of modern technology not including some way to purchase such personal items in complete anonymity. She poked the key in the van's lock. Her neck prickled. Again she felt those prying eyes drilling into her. Why couldn't she spot their source?

Trembling, she hopped into the van, locked the doors and moments later pulled warily into traffic. But if someone was following, she couldn't pinpoint him or her. She picked Beth up at the clinic. The dialysis had drained her of energy, and Eden was just as glad she didn't have to keep up a conversation with Beth during the ride home.

Although she stopped several times and let all the traffic behind them pass, she couldn't shake the sensation that someone was following them. She considered calling David but decided there was no sense worrying him without better cause than a "sensation." Besides, maybe he was already at the lake house.

But he wasn't, and even getting safely through the gate didn't steady her nerves. Leery, Eden entered the house and did a quick search that culminated in a second-floor bedroom overlooking the back of the lot, the fence and the road. No one had followed them. No one had entered the house while they were gone. Relief spilled through her. They were safe here. At least for one more night.

Beth broke into her thoughts. "I don't want to sleep on that sofa tonight. Do you suppose we could have one of these bedrooms?"

"Since we're going to be here for a while, I'd say that was a good idea. We just have to make the beds. There are sheets and blankets in the linen closet. Which one do you want?"

"The one that overlooks the lake."

"Great. I want this one." She glanced again at the back side of the lot, the fence and the road.

"David can have the one in between us," Beth said. "Now, if you won't miss me, I'm going to make my bed and take a nap."

"Sure, go ahead, sweetie. I'll check on you later."

Eden made up David's bed and her own, then returned to the van and unloaded the luggage, finally bringing in her makeup bag and the brown paper sack she'd purchased at the drugstore.

She entered the big upstairs bathroom, a room done in more oak with a color scheme of forest green and deep wine. She strolled barefoot over the fluffy rug, turned on the shower, then read and followed the instructions on the package she'd purchased.

Minutes later she stood, wrapped in a towel, still dripping wet from her shower, staring at the plastic tip of the tester.

Blue.

She was pregnant.

She sank to the toilet seat, clutching the towel around her. At least six weeks along, she realized. Shock shivered through her. She supposed at some other time she'd feel overjoyed, but how could she now?

She had no way of knowing whether the child's father was David ... or Peter.

An even worse thought struck her. Who had been watching her in the drugstore? Who else knew she might be pregnant?

Chapter Nine

As David left downtown Seattle, the freeway was heavy with the last of the rush-hour traffic. He poked Redial on the cellular phone. It was a quarter past six. He'd tried calling Eden twice since leaving the hospital ten minutes earlier and he was starting to worry.

She answered on the second ring, her voice sending a rush of relief through him. Tapping his brake, he eased into the adjoining lane. "Where are you?"

"The lake house."

He breathed easier. "Everything went smoothly, then?"

"As silk." Something in her tone belied her words, rekindling his worry.

"Then what's wrong?"

"Nothing."

David wasn't convinced. "No one followed you home?"

"No. Believe me, I made triple certain."

"That's my girl." Why, then, did she sound upset? Not that knowing Rose Hatcher was on the loose didn't have his nerves twisted, but Eden had shown no signs of distress when he'd left her at Valerie's. Had Valerie done something to rattle her?

Eden interrupted the thought. "We've established where I am, what about you?"

"I'm near my house here in town. I was longer at the hospital than I'd anticipated. But I should be with you in about an hour, hour and a half at most."

"Will you call me back when you leave there?"

He hesitated. Was that what had her worried—that something would happen to him at his house? It made sense. "I'll call as soon as I start out."

Deciding he should heed her concerns, he dropped the phone on the passenger seat and drove down his street studying every parked car. He knew his neighbors' vehicles by sight, and there wasn't one he couldn't identify.

His attention shifted to his house. It sprawled on the corner lot like a sleeping *Tyrannosaurus rex,* its pale clapboard skin lifeless in the harsh afternoon sun. A shiver worked down his spine, and he wondered at his fanciful thoughts. It was only a house, not a monster lying in wait for him.

He parked the car, then headed to his mailbox and scooped out two days' worth of bills. Inside, the house smelled stale, closed up. He carried the mail to the bedroom he'd set up as a home office and dumped it on the cluttered desk that he'd arranged in the center of the room facing the window. Afternoon sunlight filtered through the ivory miniblinds, lifting dust motes from the oak floor.

The blinker on his answering machine told him he had three calls. He'd check them later. Right now he wanted a shower and some clean clothes.

Minutes later, hot water pouring over his skin, he thought of Eden and the awful mess he'd dragged her into. She deserved better. But guilt was far from all he felt for Eden. The longing to make love to her was both an aching physical need and a spiritual desire to connect their souls. He couldn't do anything about the second need, but the first was controllable. He shifted the nozzle until cold water streamed from the spout, cooling his passion, chilling his body.

Shivering, he turned off the water, dried and dressed. He gathered his soiled clothes into a damp towel, carried it to the hamper and dropped the bundle inside. It hit the empty bottom with a thump that jarred loose a memory. There ought to be a green polo shirt at the bottom of the hamper. It wasn't there now. Had he washed it and forgotten?

He shook his head, unable to recall. The hell with that now. More-pressing matters than a dirty shirt deserved his attention. But as he shaved and combed his hair, it occurred to him there was something important that he ought to recall; try as he might, it eluded him.

In his bedroom, he pulled his gym bag from the closet and plunked it onto his unmade bed. Immediately his memories of sharing this bed with Eden shoved other images and concerns from his head, spiraling his desire for her to new heights. He stood transfixed, recalling every delicate inch of her, reliving every shattering pleasure she'd given him, realizing he was seriously in love.

The house creaked. David jerked, glancing instinctively toward the open door and into the hallway beyond. Had he heard a footstep? Or just one of the settling groans the house often made? His heart hammered against his ribs. A second passed. Then two. No one leapt out to startle him, and he laughed at himself. He was frittering away precious time scaring up ghosts that didn't exist and mooning about Eden when he could be with her.

He stuffed enough clothes in the gym bag for a few days; the lake house had a washer and dryer if their stay stretched beyond that. Packed and ready, he rechecked the house, assuring himself that windows and doors were locked.

In his home office, he hitched his hip on his desk, caught up the telephone receiver and called Eden again. "Hi. I'm on my way."

"Oh, good." A relieved sigh rushed down the line and into his ear. "Be careful."

Her voice still held that shaken quality. He scrambled for a reason. "How's Beth?"

"Tired. She's napping."

Eden had to be exhausted, too. Perhaps that was producing the quavery tone in her voice. "You know, that sounds like a great idea. Maybe you should rest awhile, too."

"Maybe I will."

"And don't worry about dinner. I'll bring something."

He hung up and punched the Rewind button on his answering machine, absently glancing at the mail he'd brought in. A plain white, legal-size envelope with typed lettering and no return address caught his attention. He tugged open the top desk drawer and scanned its contents. Where was the letter opener Colleen had given him? The thing was solid brass and resembled a Spanish dagger in shape and size. It was usually easy to spot.

It wasn't there. Damn. What had he done with it? He banged the drawer shut and picked through the mess on his desk, but a voice issuing from his answering machine paralyzed his limbs.

"Please, pick up the phone. Dr. Coulter, please. You have to help me. I swear I didn't kill Marianne. Please, pick up the phone!"

Rose Hatcher.

Cold sweat broke over David's body. As if in slow motion, he pivoted. His gaze was riveted on the black box emitting the hated voice. His pulse thundered in his ears.

"Please, Dr. Coulter. I'm innocent."

Her voice jarred his senses like the keening of a wounded animal, dredging to memory the reporter claiming that Rose had recanted her confession. The machine rolled to the next message. Also from Rose. As was the third. With each her frustration increased... as did her demands to know where he was.

David rammed his trembling hand through his hair and swore. When had she called? His machine wasn't one that automatically recorded the time calls were received.

He listened to the tape two more times. She sounded so sincere. He recalled the kind of student she'd been, and his old doubts surfaced. Was he wrong about her? Was she innocent? His faltering confidence in his ability to judge people niggled him. Maybe he was a fool to doubt. Either way, he couldn't risk Eden's life.

He disconnected the answering machine and wound the cord around it. Did the phone company have records of incoming calls? He didn't know. But it was certain Kollecki couldn't dismiss this tape. It was proof Rose Hatcher wasn't in California.

As he started out of his office, an awful thought struck him, and he cursed again. He'd changed his home phone number after Rose's trial. How had she gotten his new number? It was unlisted.

His gut clenched. The only way she could have gotten his telephone number was if she'd somehow gotten into his house. But that was impossible ... wasn't it?

He thought again of the missing polo shirt, and the hair on his nape lifted. He darted a glance over his shoulder, suddenly uneasy in his own home. Was he alone? Had he, after all, heard a footstep earlier? Hell, why hadn't he changed the locks when he'd changed his phone number?

EDEN AWAKENED from her nap to find the house dark and the hour nearing ten. She sprang up on the bed and immediately went to the windows. Worry squirmed through her. Where was David? His car was not parked out back beside her van. Why hadn't he called?

She turned to the telephone lying on the bedside table. As she started toward it, it rang. Eden jumped, then quickly answered it. "David?"

He assured her it was indeed him, then apologized for not calling sooner but said that he was okay and would explain what had happened when he arrived, which should be in the next two minutes.

She was downstairs when his headlights swept across the living-room windows. As glad as Eden was that he was safe and sound and here, she dreaded facing him ... armed with the knowledge of her pregnancy.

Not that she intended to tell him. Not yet, anyway. It was still too new to her. Too unexpected. She had to get used to the idea herself before sharing it with anyone.

With his entrance, he brought the sense-tangling fragrance of his cologne and the mouth-watering aroma of

Mexican food. Her stomach growled in anticipation, and Eden found she was actually famished.

Further proof of her condition. Sick in the morning, ravenous at night—symptoms she'd heard described by mothers-to-be at baby showers she'd attended in the good old days when she'd had girlfriends. Before Peter. How she longed for a close female friend she could turn to at times like these, someone who understood her fears and the secret joy she felt—despite not knowing who the father was or what the future held—for the new life growing within her.

Fearing that joy would somehow be conveyed in her eyes or her expression, Eden kept her face averted as she took the bags of food from him and carried them into the kitchen.

David followed, going to the cupboards and bringing plates and silverware to the table. "Beth still asleep?"

"Yes, I'll wake her in a few minutes." Eden pulled the containers from the sacks and glanced at the man she loved. There was an easiness between them similar to what her parents had shared. This was the home life she'd longed for and never had.

His green eyes turned toward her, and she realized she was fooling herself. This was a false comfort—as fragile as the containers holding their food. "Are you going to tell me what kept you?"

He grew thoughtful, and Eden tensed, knowing instinctively that the delay had had something to do with Rose.

"I went to see Kollecki." David expected this news to jar Eden.

Instead, her only visible reaction was a slight lift of her eyebrows . . . as if she didn't care. "What about?"

He disliked the lines of tension around her eyes. Had she slept? Or had something kept her awake? "Are you sure nothing happened to upset you today?"

Eden nearly spilled the fried rice she was scooping onto her plate. Should she tell him about the drugstore stalker? No. Then she'd have to explain what she'd been doing at the drugstore. "Nothing, I swear."

Why didn't he believe her? He arched an eyebrow and studied her precious face, but she didn't look at him, concentrating instead on filling her plate as if it were some lifesaving task.

Apparently she had no intention of telling him whatever it was. Well, he could be patient. He filled his own plate, then started again where he'd left off. "I went to see Kollecki because after I talked to you, I played the three messages on my answering machine. All were from Rose Hatcher."

Eden's head snapped up, her preoccupation momentarily forgotten. She scowled. "I knew it had something to do with her. What did she want?"

Between bites of food, he explained about changing his home phone number and that he'd concluded Rose could only have gotten his number by somehow gaining entrance or access to his house and looking at the telephone.

"Or maybe," Beth began as she strolled into the room. Although it was obvious that she wasn't feeling one hundred percent, she did appear rested. "Maybe she got the number somehow from your office at the medical center."

He hadn't thought of that. "I'd prefer that to images of her wandering my house."

Eden glanced up from her plate. "What did Kollecki say when he heard the tape?"

David grimaced. "His first reaction was that she could have called from California. But when I told him about changing my phone number after her trial and that she'd have no way of getting my new number if she were in California, he looked as if he had a mouthful of sour grapes."

Beth laughed. Eden barely cracked a smile. David wanted to pull her close and ease whatever worry had her in its grip. At least her appetite seemed to have returned. He decided now was not the time to mention that what had probably made Kollecki listen was his missing shirt and letter opener.

Beth insisted on hearing about the answering-machine tape, and as David repeated his story, Eden caressed her stomach with tenderness. How long before she would show? How long before this pregnancy would no longer be her secret? She frowned as she chewed her enchilada. The most worrisome thought was that Rose already knew about the baby. Eden shuddered inside. What would that knowledge mean to Rose?

Panic seized her. Maybe she should just leave. Disappear in the night. But how could she? Rose Hatcher was out there, waiting for her to make a wrong move. To panic. And panic was Eden's enemy as much as Rose was.

"Eden, are you okay?" Beth asked.

Eden started from the thoughts and glanced at Beth. "I'm fine, sweetie. Just a little tired."

She didn't want either of them studying her too closely at the moment. She shifted her gaze to David and made an effort to contribute to the conversation. "What's Kollecki going to do?"

"He contacted the King County police, and starting tonight, they'll watch my house."

"Are they going to protect us, too?" Beth's appetite was also better than it had been this morning. She focused on David for an answer.

He shook his head. "And admit he was wrong about Eden?"

"Why is he so intractable? The police are supposed to protect innocent people."

Eden sighed. "Tenacity is a good attribute in a cop— unless you're the target of that tenacity. And Kollecki doesn't think I'm innocent."

A new fear slithered through Eden. What would happen to her baby if Kollecki somehow managed to put her back in jail? The urge to take off for parts unknown clutched her anew. But one glance at her sister and she knew she'd never try running away. Until Beth had her new kidney, she was as trapped as a rat in a laboratory maze. One wrong turn and Rose Hatcher would pounce.

David shoved his plate aside. "Let's look on the bright side. With the police watching my house, if Rose shows up, she'll be caught."

Beth's eyes rounded. "Do you really think she'll be caught that easily?"

Eden smiled wryly. "I agree. Life is seldom that simple." Besides, David wasn't taking everything into account. "You said Rose recanted her confession."

"Yes." He nodded, then told her that the reporter at the hospital had mentioned it to him even before he'd heard it for himself.

"Kollecki says it's a ploy. According to him, every prisoner claims they were wrongly convicted."

"I suppose." Eden wondered. *She* was innocent and, above all else, she had to prove it. Could Rose Hatcher feel the same? As farfetched as it seemed, could Rose also be innocent? Eden dropped her napkin onto her plate, stood and began gathering the dirty dishes.

David scooted back in his chair and stretched. Something in his pants pocket poked his hipbone. He withdrew a long white envelope, frowning. "What the...?"

Then he recalled. This was the letter he'd been about to open at his house when he'd heard the message from Rose.

"What's that?" Beth peered over his shoulder.

"Don't know. Came in the mail. No return address, but it was mailed in Seattle." He pried the flap up at one corner, then jerked his finger through the top of the envelope, ripping it jaggedly. It contained a single slip of pink stationery paper with a white rose embossed along the top edge.

Beth gasped. Eden turned from the sink, her alarm telescoping across the room. David smoothed the paper with tremulous fingers, his mouth as dry as the torn envelope.

The typewritten message was short and to the point.

David darling,
How can you cast my love aside as though it means nothing to you? I beg of you, please, come to your senses. Give up on Eden ... before it's too late!!!

The heat drained from his face. Every time he felt as if the woman would be caught and out of their lives forever, she reappeared like some evil apparition.

THE WOMAN STEERED her car swiftly past the street-lights on the Mercer Island road. Had David gotten her note yet? He was being stubborn. But she would give him a little more time. Not much, though. A couple of days. After that he would have no one to blame but himself. His life, his destiny, his future, were in his hands. If he made the wrong choice, sadly he would pay the price.

She passed his street and parked one block over. It was after ten, the night as warm and dark as her thoughts of David. She was dressed entirely in black leather, the clothing sticking to her skin with a layer of sweat, but she didn't care. She felt as elusive as a shadow. Knowing she was nearly undetectable, she slipped silently into the dense shrubbery and tripped along the shortcut she'd discovered last year that emerged directly across from David's house.

She left the path and checked the road for prying eyes. No one seemed to be nosing about. Her attention shifted to David's house. A single night-light glowed in the kitchen window—a little beacon, inviting. She grinned, tempted... perhaps if David were home, she would use her key and go inside, join him in his bed, let him make glorious love to her.

The sound of a car passing nearby sent her ducking back into the trees. How could she let herself lose control? This was not a night for fantasies. The car and its occupants pulled into the garage of the house next to David's. The moment peace again reigned over the neighborhood, she zipped across the street, ran to a corner of David's house, pressed her body against the rough siding.

But she couldn't chase the questions from her head. Where was David? With Eden, no doubt. An image of Eden filled her head, and fury seared her insides. What had that witch been doing looking at home pregnancy tests?

All afternoon she'd had to deal with the awful possibility that Eden was pregnant with David's child. Again the horrid thought resounded through her head. The woman jammed her gloved palms against her ears to shut out the awful roaring.

She was going to have David's children. No one else. She drew a ragged breath. Unless David made a wrong choice. Then no one would be having his children. Tears filled her eyes, and a sob filled her chest. No. That possibility was too sad to consider. He would come to his senses.

She would just have to get rid of Eden permanently. And she knew exactly how to draw her out of hiding. A sly grin tugged at the woman's mouth but quickly fled as she thought how close she'd come to Eden today. Too bad that other interfering witch had looked right at her as she'd cruised the street.

Satisfaction brought the grin back. Such a small annoyance was no match for her. She had taken bigger risks, rid this world of bigger pests. The woman shoved the thought aside and crept closer to the porch, hugging the shadows near the house.

Across the street, a dog began to bark. She froze. Her chest squeezed with fear.

A man shouted, "Shut up!"

The dog's yapping ceased.

Weak in the knees, she closed the gap to the porch. She pulled the delicate item from her purse, laid it on the welcome mat and hurried off the way she'd come.

An hour later, a King County patrolman shone his flashlight across the front of David's house, caught sight of something on the front stoop and walked closer. In the beam of his light was a single white rose.

Chapter Ten

"Warm night." David approached Eden cautiously. After cleaning the kitchen and seeing that Beth made it to bed, she'd been preoccupied. She'd wandered out to the deck about half an hour ago. Deciding she needed to sort out whatever was bothering her, he'd left her alone. But the night was too inviting to stay indoors. "Hard to believe September is only a week away, isn't it?"

"Uh-huh," she murmured, glancing up at the sky.

At half past midnight, the full moon hovered overhead like a huge spotlight surrounded by twinkling stars and cast a luminous glow across the water.

Boyhood memories of summers spent swimming in this lake late at night with James and Great-Uncle Harry stirred in David. He set his coffee cup on the picnic table and joined Eden on the wooden bench, sitting backward so he could look at the lake.

She glanced over at him and smiled. "It's so quiet here—a person could almost get lost in the peacefulness of it."

He leaned his elbows on the table, his back pressed to its edge, and listened to the night sounds, the distant croaking of frogs and the occasional muted splash of a fish or an otter. "When Great-Uncle Harry was alive, James and I used to spend a week or two every summer out here. Camping on the lawn. Skinny-dipping after midnight."

"Lucky you. My family's idea of a summer holiday was a week or two in some big city, touring every museum and historical monument we could pack into our schedule. The closest we came to nudity was a Gaugin."

The regret in her voice tugged at his heart.

He quirked an eyebrow at her. "You mean to say you've never gone skinny-dipping?"

Eden looked amused. "'Fraid not."

"Of course. That explains your stunted psyche. Fortunately we can remedy the problem right now." He caught her by the arm, lifting her to her feet. "Come on."

"Where?"

"To the lake, of course."

"David," she protested, struggling to free herself from his grasp. "Get serious."

"I am serious. Seriously crazy about you." He stopped and pulled her against him.

Her head gently collided with his solid midriff. The warmth of his body was welcome, reassuring, loving. She circled her arms around his narrow waist. He lowered his head until his lips hovered a breath away from her ear. "Come swim with me, my love?"

Awash in the wonderful feel of him, Eden laughed and a titillating thrill whisked through her, brushing the dark worries from her mind. Somehow he always made her cares less weighty, always made her smile. "Won't it be cold?"

"Cold? Naw, let's say... refreshing."

The thought of actually doing something so decadent, so impulsive, so freeing, kindled a fire in her, an urge to rebel against the conventions that heretofore she'd followed her whole life. And why not? Swimming wouldn't hurt the baby, and she had nothing else to lose...except for some long-lamented inhibitions. "Last one in is a dirty duck."

She shoved out of his arms and scurried down the six steps that led off the deck to the lawn. They ran to the dock like small children, their laughter echoing off the lake. But as David began disrobing, Eden had second thoughts. "Does James have any nosy neighbors?"

"None. You aren't chickening out, are you?"

"Chicken? I might be modest, but I'm no chicken." She was, however, amazed at the lack of self-consciousness she felt around David. She shed her skirt and blouse, then her bra and lastly her panties. David did a cannonball into the lake and came up spitting water, letting out a loud "Yahoo!"

Eden dipped her toe into the water. It was definitely cool in the warm night air, but not as bad as she'd thought it would be. She took a deep breath and eased off the dock, making a small splash and emitting a squeal of happiness.

David laughed delightedly, the sound bouncing off the water and into her heart. "Did I promise you refreshing?"

"It feels so weird, so wonderful." Eden laughed and swam toward him, draping her arms around his neck when she reached him, reveling in the warmth of his body. Her tender, taut nipples encountered his solid chest, and a delicious tingle shot through her, igniting a fierce hunger deep in her core that sent shards of desire spiraling through her.

David responded in kind, his own desire sleek and hot and hard against her belly. She cupped his face in both of her hands. His eyes glistened with passion and tenderness as soft in the moonlight as iridescent candles. He bent his mouth to hers, murmuring her name, holding them afloat with his powerful legs.

His kiss melted her insides, heating her chilled body like a tube of boiling liquid glass that begged for him to mold her to his whims. His hands slicked over her wet skin, driving her passion higher, and when he reached one hand between her legs, finding the delicate center, his finger slid easily into her.

She released a small cry of pleasure against his ear. "Oh, David, I've missed being with you."

"Me, too, love." His voice grazed her senses with its huskiness.

He gathered her thighs and lifted her legs over his hips, lowering her onto his rigid shaft. She cried out in joy as their bodies became one and locked her legs behind his back, instantly caught in his wondrous water ballet, pirouetting, lifting and gliding, weightless and serene, a ballet whose choreography bespoke legends as old and mystical as mermaids and mermen.

Their heads dipped below the surface, then broke through the water into the glorious night. Eden laughed breathlessly. David laughed, too, then his mouth was on hers again, and the dance began in earnest.

The water splashed with every lift, with every downward thrust, special music written just for this moment, played only for their ears. The tide crashed and ebbed, harder and faster until at last it burst across the shores of their souls and spilled their joy into the night air, echoing sweetly across the lake.

David released her and sank below the surface again, then came slowly out of the water and grinned at her. "My God, you're incredible."

"No, my darling, you are the incredible one." She swam closer and dragged her fingers slowly from his temple to his jaw. The wonder in his eyes humbled her and filled her with the knowledge that this man loved her as she loved him. Emotion overwhelmed her, sapping her strength. "I think we ought to get out of the water. My stamina is depleted."

He lifted her onto the dock, then pulled himself up beside her. They sat on his slacks, both a bit breathless.

David traced a finger along the edge of her kneecap. "Well, what do you think about skinny-dipping?"

Eden covered his hand with hers and grinned up at him. "If it's always this wonderful, I'm sorry I took so long to try it."

"Just don't try it like this with anyone else." He caught her against him, kissed her lightly on the mouth, then held her a moment longer. But the air was now cooler than the water and goose bumps rose on her delicate arms. "We should probably go inside."

As they started for the house, Eden's mind returned to the baby. She should tell David now, while things were so wonderful between them. But how would he react when she told him she wasn't certain whether or not he was the father? She couldn't bear the thought of hurting him. Disappointing him. Besides, she wanted this special evening to remain intact, wanted to hold it in her heart a while longer. But tomorrow she would have to tell him.

THE MORNING DAWNED to cloudy skies and the threat of rain. Eden lifted her head off the pillow, and her stomach heaved. She hurried to the bathroom, realizing she wouldn't have to tell David anything if he heard her being sick every morning. If she kept refusing breakfast of any kind.

She dressed in blue jeans and a cornflower blue fisherman's sweater that hung to her hips. She fussed with her hair and covered her pallor with a light layer of makeup and rouge, then relinquished the bathroom to Beth.

David was at the kitchen table, sipping coffee and munching toast. He wore black Levi's and a forest green sweatshirt that accented the green of his eyes. His chocolate hair lay neat against his head, a lock stealing over his high brow. He glanced up at her, a smile lighting his handsome face.

Her heart quickened, and memories of last night swirled through her mind. But she reined them in. She had to tell him about the baby. Now. While Beth was showering. Her palms felt damp. "Hi, there."

"Hi, there, yourself." He started to stand. "Want some coffee?"

"No, thanks." She motioned him back into his seat and took the one opposite. She had to see his face as she told him. She drew a steadying breath and folded her hands on the table in front of her. "David, I—"

The ringing of his cellular phone cut her off. She sank back in the chair as he answered.

"Dr. Coulter." There was a pause. David heard breathing and for a tense second wondered if Rose Hatcher had somehow gotten his cell phone number.

But he was wrong. "Coulter. This is Detective Kollecki."

The man hadn't needed him to identify himself. The "Coulter" had been enough. David was getting to know and dread that voice.

"What's up, Detective?" David glanced at Eden, seeing the slight tensing of her body. He reached across the table and placed his hand over hers.

Kollecki said, "I was wondering if you and Mrs. Prescott could come to the station this morning."

"Why?" He sat straighter. Was this good news? "Did the King County cops find Rose at my house?"

"I don't know that they found anything at your house." Kollecki sounded as if he didn't know what David was talking about. "This is another matter altogether."

David frowned and pulled his hand from Eden's. What game was Kollecki playing now? "Why don't you just tell me what it is now and save us the hassle?"

"Not over the telephone, sir." Kollecki paused. "Could you make it by eleven?"

An hour from now. David let out an exasperated breath. "Fine. We'll be there."

He disconnected. A bad feeling churned through his gut and crept along his nerves.

"What?" Eden's mouth stretched thin, her eyes rounding with dread.

Was she responding to his expression? He shook off his worried scowl, shifted in his chair and caught her hands again. "I don't know. He wouldn't say. He wants us in Issaquah by eleven."

But he realized Eden was neither calmed nor fooled by his "bedside manner." She knew him too well. As if her sweater was suddenly inefficient at abating the chill in the air, she hugged herself. "Maybe I should call my attorney."

"Whoa. Let's see what this is about first." He raised his hands, palms toward her, in a slow-down gesture. Her suggestion might inflame the situation unnecessarily. "You can always call from the station, if need be. But I don't think we should jump to conclusions. Especially awful ones. For all we know, it's nothing more than something about the tape from my answering machine.

"Unless—" his face brightened "—unless Rose has been captured, and Kollecki wants to apologize to you in person."

"I don't think I'll hold my breath." But she had to admit it would be a sweet ending to the hell Kollecki had put her through the past seven weeks.

The sound of the shower shutting off upstairs brought home another concern.

"What about Beth? I don't want her at the police station, and I don't like leaving her alone when we aren't sure how long we'll be."

"My darling mother hen, your chick is twenty-three. We'll leave her the other cell phone. She can call if she needs us. Or if the hospital contacts her about a donor."

Eden nodded, chagrined. She couldn't help mothering Beth; she'd raised her since she was fourteen. Would she ever let Beth grow up all the way?

But Beth was already halfway there. And when they told her the news, Beth was more concerned about what Kollecki wanted with Eden and David than about staying alone. David told her he was certain it had to do with the tape he'd taken to Kollecki yesterday. That seemed to satisfy her.

"You'd better get going, then. And don't frown, Eden. I'll be fine," Beth assured her. "I have my beeper, and I don't plan to do anything more strenuous than feeding the ducks and reading my book and resting. Pretty harmless pastimes.''

IF ONLY KOLLECKI WERE harmless, Eden thought as he met them in the waiting area. His red hair hadn't its usual sheen, and his dark eyes seemed lost in the crevices of skin at their edges, as if he'd been up for hours or hadn't slept at all the night before. She hoped his conscience over what he'd done to her was directly responsible for any loss of sleep the man had suffered.

He ushered them through the locked doors that led to the jail, and Eden shuddered, recalling the awful nights she'd spent here and at the King County facility. They followed him past his office and toward the interrogation room Eden had been questioned in that first morning after learning of Peter's murder.

The door bumped open, and Ariel Bell stumbled out into the hallway. Twin blotches of red stung her otherwise ashen face. Mascara smudged both eyes like jagged black bruises. Seeing David and Eden, she sobbed, "Oh, God. She was just lying there. I thought at first she'd tripped and spilled coffee...or something. But when I bent to help her, I saw—I saw..." Her fisted hand fluttered to her mouth, and she stepped back, right smack into Detective Tagg. "It was blood."

"What are you talking about?" Eden gripped David's arm.

Ron Tagg said, "Please, Ms. Bell, let us handle this."

"What? Oh, of course, I'm sorry." Ariel's face grew thoughtful, and she dredged up an apologetic half smile. "I guess I'm still in shock. Not that I haven't seen dead bodies—"

"D-dead—" Eden recoiled.

"Whose body?" David demanded.

"Please." Kollecki pointed toward the interrogation room. "If you and Mrs. Prescott would just go inside, I'll explain."

David started to protest, but Kollecki's face was redder than chili powder. The detective didn't like others stealing his control of a situation, and Ariel had knocked him momentarily out of the driver's seat.

Confusion and alarm made Eden's eyes as wide as blue lakes. David guided her past the others and into the interrogation room.

Kollecki heaved his large shoulders. "Tagg, see to it someone takes Ms. Bell home."

Kollecki shut the door behind them and released a loud breath. "Please sit down."

Eden dropped onto one of the plastic chairs, but David's patience was gone. He grasped the back on the chair next to Eden. "You tell us right now what the hell is going on, Kollecki."

The red started rising in the detective's face again.

Eden reached up and gripped David's hand. "Whose body was Ariel talking about?" Her voice held none of the strength of her grip.

Detective Tagg stepped quietly into the room. For the first time, David realized the creases around Tagg's eyes were as etched as Kollecki's. "Does this have something to do with Rose Hatcher?"

Tagg shook his head. "Not that we're aware of."

"Who, then?" David's impatience echoed in the concrete-block room.

Kollecki leaned on the table, his palms flat, his gaze settled studiously on Eden. "Valerie Prescott. Ms. Bell found her around six-thirty this morning...when she arrived to pick up a check she says you left there for her.''

Eden's chest squeezed. "Valerie is . . . ?"

David covered her hand with his and stared at Tagg.

Tagg nodded. "I'm afraid she's dead."

Eden gasped.

David shook his head. "D-dead?"

"But she seemed fine when I left yesterday," Eden whispered, disbelief spinning through her. "How? What happened?"

Kollecki narrowed his eyes at her. "She was murdered."

Eden's hand went to her mouth. Suddenly she remembered Ariel ranting about blood. "Shot, like Peter?"

"No." Tagg ran his hand over his silver crew cut. "Stabbed."

"But like your husband's murder, the weapon is once again missing from the crime scene." Kollecki shifted his gaze to David. "The M.E. says it was something with a blade duller than a knife . . . but shaped like a dagger."

David's eyes widened. "You think she was killed with my letter opener?"

Kollecki stepped back, adopting an innocent expression that immediately brought to mind a benevolent Santa. "I didn't say that, but I have to wonder why you brought it up."

"You implied it."

Kollecki wiped his whiskered jaw with his hand. "From where I'm sitting, it sounds to me as if you'd like me to believe it. You're the one who claims you had such a letter opener. The one who claims it's missing."

"Claims?"

"Well, look at it from my point of view, Doc. I have no proof that it was stolen. Only your word."

"There are far too many coincidences in this case for you to keep ignoring," David growled between clenched teeth.

"See, that's the thing about coincidences—in my experience, most of them aren't."

David drew in a steadying breath. Kollecki wasn't a fool, just dogged. There had to be some way of convincing him to consider even the unproved evidence.

"My letter opener *is* missing, but—" David broke off and reappraised the hard glint in the cop's small, dark eyes. "Are you accusing me of killing Valerie Prescott?"

"I'm not charging anyone at this juncture."

Tagg intervened. "We do need to know where you both were between three and eight yesterday afternoon."

"If you can alibi each other," Kollecki said, his smile cold, "then you don't have anything to worry about, do you?"

Eden glanced at David, regretting her insistence that they run their errands separately yesterday. David could account for his time until around six. But although she'd spoken to him after that, he'd called from his cell phone, and she realized with sickening clarity that he could have been calling from anywhere.

She had no better alibi. She could account for her time from five-thirty on, but earlier she'd been alone, driving and at the drugstore. Would that snail of a salesclerk recall her asking for the brown paper bag?

David patted her arm. "Don't say another word. Not without your attorney."

"You might want to call a lawyer, too, Dr. Coulter," Tagg said.

Kollecki glared at his partner. Tagg would likely get a dressing-down later, but right now David was in the hot seat.

"I checked with King County after I talked to you this morning." Kollecki's voice was deceptively soft. "It seems a patrolman found a white rose on your porch last night."

David blanched.

Kollecki folded his hands over his belly. "I know you'd have me believe some woman left it after killing Ms. Prescott, but I have to ask myself what proof there is of that. What proof is there that you didn't leave it there yourself, Doc?"

David bit down his fury, clamping his mouth shut, knowing Kollecki was purposefully provoking him, was hoping he'd say something incriminating. "I'd like to call my lawyer."

Kollecki didn't like it, but he respected the law too much to deny them their rights. Eden called her attorney and then Beth and told her this would take longer than they'd originally thought, stalling Beth's questions by promising she'd explain when she got home.

While she waited for her attorney, Eden was kept separated from David. Her head ached, and her body felt numb. She hadn't been fond of Valerie, but her murder shocked and saddened Eden.

She felt better having her lawyer present as she gave her statement and better yet when she was allowed to leave and was reunited with David. The dark clouds overhead leaked the first few raindrops as they hurried hand in hand to his car.

Neither noticed the black compact pull out of the busy parking lot two cars behind them.

Chapter Eleven

David and Eden left Issaquah in silence, the car's tires slurping over the rain-bathed road, punctuating the tension inside the vehicle. The past few hours had left Eden numb, drained and awash in questions.

"Maybe you should call Beth," David interrupted her thoughts. "Let her know we're on our way."

"I should have done that first thing. She's probably wondering why we're so late." She hit the Redial button on the cellular phone and listened to the beeps as the call was put through. The phone rang and rang. Eden crooked her head at David. "That's odd. She's not answering. Where could she be?"

"In the bathroom? Asleep?" David grinned wryly and patted her leg. "Out feeding the ducks?"

"In the rain?"

"It might not be raining at the lake yet."

"That's true." Eden pursed her lips. "I'm mother-henning again, aren't I?"

"Who can blame you?"

She knew he was referring to what they'd just learned about Valerie, but she appreciated his consideration in not saying it aloud. She didn't want to talk about Val. Didn't want to think about telling Beth. Or how devastated Beth would be. Hell, she didn't want to think about Val, period. Not dead. Murdered. But she couldn't seem to stop. "David, what was all that business about your letter opener?"

"I should have told you last night." His mouth stretched into a tight line, and a muscle jumped in his neck. She knew the possibility that his letter opener had been used to kill Valerie was eating at him. He sighed, then explained how he'd discovered it was missing. Along with his shirt. "Kollecki was right. I can't prove either was stolen. I couldn't even find where anyone had broken into my house."

A chilling idea struck Eden. "Could Rose have a key?"

"I admit that crossed my mind. I'm having the locks changed as soon as possible." He clicked the windshield wipers from intermittent to constant. "In fact, I've given Rose a lot of thought and I can't understand why she would kill Valerie. Shannon and Marianne fit a pattern consistent with her obsession disorder, but Valerie doesn't."

Eden's insides were a mass of jelly. He'd hit on something that had also been nagging her for the past hour. Motive. What could Rose have had against Valerie? Why would anyone murder her? "I had Val at the top of our suspect list before we learned about Rose's escape. I could see Val as a woman intent on vengeance, a woman obsessed with men she couldn't have, but not as the victim in this."

"Are we overlooking something?"

"Oh, I don't know." Eden sighed and leaned against the car seat, closed her eyes and rubbed her temples.

A memory jerked her upright. Her eyes flew open, and the seat belt dug into her tender breasts. "Yesterday, when Val helped me carry Beth's bags to the van, she said something odd."

"What?" Hope etched the single word.

Eden squeezed her eyes shut, trying to recall exactly. "She said, 'What is *she* doing here?'"

"And she didn't say who this 'she' was?"

"No. She dismissed it. But I followed the direction of her gaze to a black compact at the corner Stop sign. It was too far away and the windows were so darkly tinted, I couldn't see who was driving. Could it have been Rose?"

"Did Valerie know what Rose looked like?"

Eden thought back. "Yes. She went to her trial a couple of times."

The news surprised him. "I didn't see her there."

"I think she went because it had something to do with you."

He glanced away, uncomfortable with this knowledge. He was quiet for a moment, then said, "I can't believe the woman Valerie saw was Rose. Valerie was present at the hospital when that reporter told me Rose had escaped from jail. Val would never have so lightly dismissed spotting an escaped convict in her neighborhood."

"Never." The implication chilled Eden. "Not Valerie."

"If she didn't see Rose, then who?" He didn't like it. His doubts of Rose sprang up like a patch of bothersome weeds he could no longer ignore. "If only I could find Rose and talk to her."

The rain suddenly came down from the sky as violently and loudly as darts hitting the car. Eden's head pounded in a similar rhythm. She stared through the blinding downpour, forcing her mind to focus on the heavy traffic, on motorists driving slower than the speed limit, on anything that would keep her from contemplating David seeking out Rose for a long, possibly fatal chat.

But what if Rose was innocent? What if someone else was behind all of this? Some unknown, unsuspected someone? Eden's limbs felt as taut as piano wire, and she ached with impatience to get home and stretch, and maybe even scream in frustration, or cry for a sister-in-law who'd never liked her.

The clacking of the wipers grated on her nerves. She tried phoning Beth again, thinking she'd feel better if she could touch base with her sister. Still no answer. Her muscles tensed, and she silently berated herself for conjuring problems where none existed. *Quit mother-henning.* Beth *was* probably napping... or feeding ducks.

But like a dozen hungry mallards, disquiet pecked at her brain.

The closer they got to Lake Retreat, the less it rained. At the house, only a sprinkle fell. "Told you so," David said, driving through the gate. "All that worry for nothing."

It wasn't until Eden took one look at the lights gleaming from inside the house that she breathed easier. They'd find Beth curled on one of the sofas reading her book.

But the house was cold inside, and the sofas showed no signs of recent occupancy. Fighting the returning dismay, Eden went through the lower level quietly, not calling out in case Beth was napping. She wasn't downstairs. Eden took the stairs two at a time. Beth's bedroom was vacant, the bed made. Eden found the bathroom just as empty. Panic overtook her dismay.

"David!" she called out. "Is Beth down by the dock?"

He glanced out the kitchen window. "I don't see her."

A moment later, Eden joined him, and they hurried out to the deck, down the steps, across the lawn and to the lake, calling Beth's name. She was nowhere to be found. Eden's fear clawed her stomach. "Dear God, where is she?"

"Don't panic. Maybe the hospital called."

"Then why didn't she call us?"

"Maybe she did...when we were being questioned."

"She would have left a note."

"Probably. But call the hospital anyway."

"How would she have gotten to the hospital?"

"Beth's resourceful enough to call a cab. Please phone the hospital."

At a loss for something better to do, Eden darted back inside. David walked the perimeter of the lot and circled the house, shaking his head at Eden as he passed by the kitchen window.

Precious minutes passed before the fourth-floor desk nurse answered. Eden tapped her fingers on the counter. "Hello, yes." She identified herself and asked if perhaps Beth had been notified of a donor today.

"I'm just coming on shift, Mrs. Prescott." The voice had a flat quality and didn't belong to anyone she recognized. "But let me check."

David came inside. "She's not outside."

Eden relayed the nurse's message to him, breaking off as the flat voice once again filled her ear. "Mrs. Prescott? You still there?"

"Yes."

"Well, I'm sorry to say, there was no donor for Beth today. Maybe tomorrow."

Eden hung up. "She's not at the hospital."

The air pressed from her lungs as if a concrete block had landed on her chest. She stared out the window, her gaze transfixed on the dock as she willed Beth to materialize before her eyes. It took a second to register what else was not at the dock. She caught David's arm. "The rowboat is gone."

"Surely Beth wouldn't have gone rowing." He craned his neck, focusing on the dock. "It's too strenuous for her."

"Then give me another explanation for why that boat is missing."

He shook his head.

They raced back out into the rain that now plopped on their heads and into their eyes in huge, irritating, saturating dollops. A breeze churned the water. David arched his hand over his eyes and scanned the lake.

"There it is!" He pointed toward a distant corner where a thick clump of water lilies grew.

The boat bobbed in the rising wind. Unmanned. Looking abandoned. Adrift. Terror gripped Eden. "Oh, David, it looks empty. Beth."

David caught her by the upper arms, his hold gentle but firm. "We don't know that this means anything. You go back inside, and I'll borrow the neighbor's skiff."

"No!" She squinted against the rain. "I'm coming with you."

"All right. But go get the phone and some coats."

Minutes later they were seated in the metal skiff, David at the oars. Wind and rain blew against them, slowing their progress. Five agonizing minutes later—

although David rowed as fast as possible—they had only reached the halfway point.

Eden's gaze never left the rowboat. It twisted and her heart twisted with it. It rocked and her stomach rocked with it. What would they find? Her mind invoked one awful scenario after another. She gripped the sides of the boat harder.

David grunted, forcing the oars deeper, the skiff onward. At last they were at the lily patch, three feet from the rowboat.

"Beth?" Eden cried from a throat so tight the word came out strangled.

Wind howled like a taunting devil.

Eden couldn't breathe.

As David rowed closer, he stretched and peered over the gunwale. "She's there. In the bottom of the boat."

Eden saw first the flowered slicker she'd given Beth in her second year of college, then Beth's raven hair. She lay curled like a sleeping dog. But was she asleep? Eden's heart was in her throat. "Beth?"

Beth didn't move. Fear gripped Eden in a vise.

David shouted, "Beth!"

Beth jerked, her eyes coming slowly open. She was alive. Eden's chest heaved with relief as Beth lurched to a sitting position, fear radiating from her rounded eyes. "Eden?"

"Dear God, Beth, what happened?" Eden cried. "What are you doing out here?"

"I—I was down on the dock, feeding the ducks bread, when I heard a noise near the house. I thought it was you guys. But when I called out, I saw someone in dark clothing dive behind the trees. I'd left the telephone in the kitchen and I didn't know what to do, so I got in the boat and rowed away."

Someone had been snooping around the house? Eden's muscles ached with tension. Whoever it was had not been there when David and she had arrived home; they'd searched inside and outside and would again as soon as they were back on shore. "No one's there now. Come on, sweetie. We'll tow you back and discuss this over some hot cocoa."

"And cinnamon rolls," David added, grinning at Eden, obviously recalling the last time he'd made them for her and burned them to crisps. "Heated cinnamon rolls are my specialty."

HALF AN HOUR LATER, they not only had hot cocoa and thick, gooey, unburned cinnamon rolls, but a fire blazing in the fireplace. They were all wearing dry clothes and enjoying the sweet treat.

David set his cup on the floor and stared at the fire, but he had the air of a caged tiger.

Beth shoved her hair off her forehead. "For pity's sake, David. Just ask, okay?"

He jerked up at that, then laughed. "Have you thought of taking that mind-reading act of yours on the road?"

"Doesn't take the psychic hot line to figure out that you want to know who and what I saw."

"So spill the beans, kiddo. Could you tell whether it was a man or a woman?"

"Woman, I'd say. Do you think it was Rose?" Beth shivered.

"Are you catching cold?" Eden reached over and felt her forehead. Was it warmer than normal? "Maybe we should take you to the hospital, sweetie, and make sure you're okay."

"Oh, please," Beth lamented. "David, tell her I'm okay."

"She's okay." David winked at Eden. He could see a trip to the hospital right now might cause Beth more trauma, but Eden's concern was understandable. "Let's compromise. We'll keep close tabs on you, and if it looks necessary, then we'll make the trip. Meanwhile I prescribe bed rest."

"I accept," Beth said. "But first I want to know what Kollecki wanted with you two."

Eden tensed.

David silently signaled for her to let him handle this. Tomorrow was soon enough to tell Beth about Valerie. She wouldn't be seeing the news on television or hearing about it from any outside source. She needed a good night's sleep before she was presented more distressing news. "One of my neighbors spotted someone at my house last night and called the police. But King County didn't know where to reach me and they didn't contact Kollecki until this morning.

"Kollecki had a few more questions for me about my answering-machine tapes, then Eden and I met the King County police at my house to make certain no one had gotten in and nothing was disturbed."

Eden was amazed at how easily he lied. Amazed and grateful.

"And? *Was* anything disturbed?" Beth asked.

"Not a thing. False alarm."

"Good." Beth yawned and stretched and bade them good-night. Eden went up ten minutes later and tucked her in. She prayed Beth's ordeal wouldn't bring on nightmares.

Back downstairs, Eden rejoined David, sinking onto the sofa beside him. The fire crackled and snapped, and she couldn't keep her eyes from sliding to the windows, couldn't keep from wondering if the person Beth had seen might still be out there, hiding, watching, plotting against them.

Reflexively she inched closer to David, ever aware that the last thing she should do was allow someone obsessed with him to see them together. "Who do you think Beth saw?"

"Good question." David leaned back and stretched his arm along the top of the sofa behind her shoulders, reaching fingers to pluck at the knit of her sweater. His gaze was tender. "A couple of hours ago, I would have been certain it was Rose. Now I'm not so sure."

Eden cringed inside, her gaze stealing again to the naked windows and the black night beyond. Half expecting to see a woman's face pressed to the panes, she braced herself against certain, sudden fright. The only woman reflected in the glass was herself, a pale-faced apparition who wouldn't scare a flea. "Shouldn't we notify the police?"

"I called while you were upstairs. But they can only come out if there's been a break-in."

"Even if it might have been an escaped convict?"

"What proof do we have of that?" God knew, he'd had the police's need of physical proof rammed home enough lately to penetrate even his thick skull. "The word of an exhausted young woman?"

"Well, she saw something."

"Yeah, something. But was it a someone?"

"What are you saying?"

He sighed. "Beth has been under a great deal of stress, waiting for the kidney while getting weaker every day. Then there's been Peter's death. Your arrest. The relentless press. Knowing a stalker may be after us. Our hiding out. All of which must be preying on her mind. On her imagination. We can't swear she wasn't spooked by a neighborhood dog or the wind or shadows or all three.''

She couldn't dispute that they were all spooked, jumpy. She drew her legs tight against her chest and rested her head on her knees, considering the possibility that Beth had imagined seeing someone prowling the grounds. Eden realized, given the mood hovering around her now, *she* could probably summon a person or shadow herself. ''I guess you could be right.''

He dropped his arm around her shoulders and pulled her closer. Eden nuzzled his chest, staring at the flames glowing red and blue in the fireplace. Silence reigned for a full ten seconds, then David pulled back. ''I've also thought long and hard about something else. Rose might have killed Marianne. She might have killed Valerie. But Valerie's gun was stolen from her Mercedes three weeks before Shannon and Peter were murdered.''

''While Rose was in an Oregon jail,'' Eden finished for him. Like an awakened monster, her uneasiness stretched with new life.

She hated giving up Rose as the star player in the nightmare her life had become. It left them at square one. Frustrated. Frightened. And vulnerable to the sick fancy of an unknown adversary—whose next move could not be anticipated. She hugged her knees harder. ''Do you have any idea who it might be, then?''

''I think we need to figure that out.''

''Resurrect our suspect list?''

''Yes.''

''It was a pretty short list to start with, but now that Val—'' Her throat constricted at the thought of how

Val's innocence had been proved. "Just Denise Smalley."

"There have to be others."

Pondering the problem, she got up, went to her room and returned with a tablet and pen. She sat back down beside David and wrote "Denise Smalley" at the top of the page. Then moved the pen to the next line. "Who else?"

"Hmm . . ."

Eden tapped the pen on the paper. "Was Denise's name on that hit list found in Rose's apartment?"

"No. Why?"

"Maybe we should include the names of the women who were on that list."

David's eyebrows arched up. "Why?"

"Because if Rose didn't kill Shannon, maybe Rose didn't make up that list herself. Maybe it was planted—like the gun in my van."

His eyes widened. "You think our stalker is using the old ploy of making herself so obvious she'll automatically be eliminated from suspicion?"

"Can we afford to overlook that possibility?"

"You're suggesting Rose was framed for Marianne's murder?"

"You said she was recanting her confession, and I can't help recalling Beth's description of Rose as a person who would help a fly escape from a room rather than swat it. *Was* Rose that kind of person?"

David considered. "She was reticent and tended toward—at least I thought at the time—hero worship. For me. For Marianne. After the murder, I decided the worship was plain old jealousy." Had he been wrong about everything? Had she merely been shy, maybe docile, pliable to the point where more-determined minds than her own manipulated her? Had she been framed? Every day he was becoming more convinced of it. He made up his mind. "We can't afford to overlook the possibility that she's innocent."

He took the tablet from Eden, and below Denise's name, he wrote two other names. Eden had heard of neither woman. His hand faltered as he wrote the names of his student assistant, his secretary and Beth's nurse. She knew he couldn't comprehend any one of these three women committing the horrendous crimes that had been done in the guise of loving him, but he couldn't ignore even the slimmest of chances that they were.

Not with their own lives on the line.

He relinquished the tablet to her. "Can you think of anyone else?"

"Just one."

The telephone rang. David answered. "Dr. Coulter."

Eden wrote "Rose Hatcher" on the last line.

David stared at the name, realizing he was hearing the voice of that very woman in his ear. "Dr. Coulter, is it really you?"

A chill shot through him. "R-Rose?"

"Yeah, it's me. I tried calling you at your house, but you were never there."

The chill turned to frost. His gaze flew to the bare windows. "Where are you, Rose? Where are you calling from?"

"Oh, I can't tell you that. The police are looking for me. You probably heard I escaped, but I had to, Dr. Coulter. I didn't kill Marianne."

David snatched the pen from Eden and scrawled across the tablet for her to get the other telephone and call the police while he kept Rose talking.

Where had Beth said she'd left the other cellular phone? In the kitchen. Eden scrambled up from the sofa.

David asked, "Then why did you confess, Rose?"

"I don't know. I was just so tired, and they wouldn't let me sleep and I got so confused, I started to see in my head the way Marianne had died and I thought maybe I did do it—since I could see it. But after I got to Purdy and got some sleep and could reason again, I knew I couldn't have done what they said. I'm innocent, Dr. Coulter."

Eden scanned the kitchen counter. From the other room, she could hear David asking Rose about yesterday, about Valerie. Where was the blasted cell phone? Her stomach churned. She searched the table, the floor, the top of the microwave, the top of the refrigerator. She jerked open cupboards, then drawers. The other cell phone was not in the kitchen.

Her panicked mind spit out an answer. Beth *had* seen someone. That someone had come into the house while Beth was on the lake and taken the second cell phone.

Alarm pulled her heart into her stomach like an express elevator descending from the penthouse to the basement.

She ran back to the living room, arriving just as David asked, "Tell me something, Rose...how did you get my cellular phone number?"

But Eden feared she already knew. Rose had gotten the number from the second cell phone—by pushing Redial. David's cell phone was the only number Eden had called. That meant Rose could be close by. Right outside. Watching them.

She scribbled this onto the tablet.

David frowned, then shook his head. He scrawled "Forgot," then pointed to the corner plug. The second cellular telephone was ensconced in the battery charger. Relief nearly buckled her knees. Rose did not have the phone. She was not outside.

Eden hurried to the phone and jerked it from the charger. Her hands shook so hard it took two tries to jam the battery in place.

"Never mind," David said, frustration ringing in his voice. "She hung up."

"I'm sorry. Beth said she'd left the phone in the kitchen and when I couldn't find it..." She clamped her hands on the sides of her head. "God, I actually thought someone had taken it. I'm losing my rationality."

He put his telephone down and closed the gap between them. "No more so than I. I actually suggested the police could trace a call from my cellular phone." He laughed at himself.

Eden laughed, too, her tension fragmenting. "Did Rose say where she got your cellular number?"

"No, but as Beth suggested, she could have gotten into my office at the hospital at any time that Lynzy or Colleen were out running errands and found where it's written down."

Eden handed him the cell phone. "Did Rose say where she was?"

"She wasn't about to divulge that." He squatted and replaced the phone in the charger.

Not wanting to give up on locating Rose, Eden asked, "While you were talking to her, did you hear any background noises?"

His chin jerked up, and his eyes settled on her, amusement in their mossy depths. "Like they do on TV?"

"Well..."

A lazy grin tugged at his sensuous mouth, and he unbent his body, rising slowly, grazing his fingertips up the sides of her as he stood. "Good thought, Mrs. Columbo, but I'm afraid I didn't hear a thing that would help us locate her whereabouts."

"What did she say?" Her voice was breathy.

"Same thing as on the tape. That she was innocent and I had to believe her. Help her prove it."

"And...?"

He shrugged and pulled her against his side, leading her back to the sofa. "We know she couldn't have stolen the gun, but how can I be certain about Marianne?"

"You're a great judge of character. What's your gut tell you about that?"

David's sigh was heavy as if from the weight of an onerous burden. "One of my first patients had me convinced she was suffering schizophrenia. It turned out she was an actor hired by an ex-fraternity brother of mine to play a joke on me."

"That's awful."

"I suppose I deserved it. I was pretty self-important and cocky at the time, and the joke served to bring me down a couple of well-deserved pegs. It also undermined my confidence in my ability to read people."

Eden could see what this confession cost him and realized he probably hadn't told anyone else. She also sensed he would construe any sympathy over this matter as pity, so she offered none. She grabbed his hand. "If it makes you feel any better, I've never met Rose, but I've also wondered if she's innocent. I can certainly empathize with her desire to prove it and get her life back."

Snuggled together, they discussed the women on their list for another hour. The fire was winding down, and the aura in the room felt mellow. His head was on her shoulder, his warm breath caressing her neck, the ambience between them intimate. There would be no better time to tell him about the baby.

But she couldn't bear to look at him, couldn't bear to see the possible rejection in his eyes. She drew a deep breath, releasing it with a hesitancy that mirrored her reluctance. "David, I've been putting off something that you have every right to know."

She clamped her lips together, holding her breath, waiting for his cue to continue. Silence. Then a soft snore. She crooked her neck and glanced sideways at him. He'd fallen asleep.

Disappointed yet oddly relieved, she eased out from under him, and he sank slowly to the sofa. She stood staring down at him, wondering if the baby she carried was his, if it would look like him. Smiling at the warm notion, she lifted his legs and covered him with a comforter. Then she went upstairs to bed.

THE NEXT MORNING, the rain was gone. The warmer air hitting the damp ground lifted steamy patches over the grass and soil like an eerie fog. Eden and Beth were in the kitchen and David was showering when the front door banged open and a woman called out, "Yoo-hoo! Anybody here?"

Nervous alarm gripped Eden as she made her way to the foyer, with Beth close on her heels. A silver-haired woman of ample proportions stood in the foyer, her arms weighted down with a knitting bag and a huge purse. Eden stepped protectively in front of Beth. "May I help you?"

Beyond the woman, Eden saw a motor home parked next to her van. A man with a leathery face was un-hitching a compact car from the trailer hitch.

"Well, hello. I'm Bertha McFadden. You two must be friends of James."

"Y-yes," Eden stammered.

David came down the stairs, capturing the woman's attention. "Oh, Dr. David. How are you?"

"Fine, Bertha. I trust your summer has been a great one as usual." He didn't wait for an answer but introduced Eden and Beth to the woman, explaining that Bertha and Mac were James's renters. He said to Bertha, "James wasn't expecting you for another week."

"Lordy, don't I know it, but Mac's gout was pestering him somethin' awful, and he wanted to see his doctor. But now, don't you go frettin' about us. We'll just stay in the motor home until you're gone."

"That's very kind of you." David and Eden exchanged glances. "We could use a day or two to figure out where we want to go."

Mac McFadden, his skin as dark as a coffee bean, his hair as silver as a polished dime, trudged up the steps, carrying a brown grocery sack. He was built like a Marine. Bertha spun toward him. "Mac, put that stuff back in the Winnebago. Dr. David is staying in the house for a few days."

Mac set the sack on the porch and wiped his forehead with a pristine white hankie. "Hey, Doc. Sorry to show up unannounced."

"It's no problem." David introduced Beth and Eden to Mac.

Eden said, "Why don't you come in? We have a fresh pot of coffee brewed."

"And warm cinnamon rolls," David added.

Mac's face brightened. "I've had enough coffee this morning to float a carrier ship, but I can't resist your cinnamon rolls, Doc."

Mac started forward, then stopped and stared down at something hidden by Bertha's girth on the porch. "You know better than to go stomping around without your glasses on, Bert." He glanced up at them. "She can't see two feet in front of her without them."

"What are you jawing about, Mac?" Bertha moved aside, giving them all a clearer view of the porch.

Mac pointed down. "There. You smashed to smithereens the pretty white rose that was lying on the welcome mat."

Chapter Twelve

Mac scooped up the destroyed rose. Shunning his grasp, the white petals fell apart, fluttered through the air and landed at Eden's feet. She jumped back as if they were a nest of deadly spiders. Heat drained from her face. Her heart thudded.

Bertha squatted and reached for the scattered petals. "Oh, my, I'm a clumsy old fool. Lookit what I've done to your lovely rose. I can't blame you for being angry, dear."

She lifted the petals to Eden.

Eden recoiled.

David intervened. "Don't worry about it. It's no loss to us. We don't know how the flower came to be on the porch."

But they did know, Eden thought. *She* put it there. She'd found them.

Her expression clouded with uncertainty, Bertha's eyes narrowed at Eden. "If you say so, Dr. David."

Eden shook herself, embarrassed to have treated this jolly woman so poorly. Even Mac was frowning at her. They had been out of town when she'd been arrested, and hadn't shown the slightest recognition of her, couldn't know what she'd been through or why a single flower would turn her insides to mush. "Please forgive my rudeness. Lately I've grown quite allergic to white roses."

Bertha's eyebrows shot up. "Just the white ones?"

"Yes," Eden answered, gesturing toward the kitchen. "Come on, the rolls are getting cold."

"Can't have that." Mac caught Bertha by the arm and came inside, shutting the door behind them.

"And we gotta phone Mac's doctor," Bertha said.

The next hour passed unbearably slowly for Eden. There wasn't enough coffee and cinnamon rolls in the world to alleviate the horror at finding yet another rose. She could no more follow the conversation than she could answer all the questions somersaulting through her mind. Had the stalker left the rose as a warning that she knew where they were? Or because she'd killed again?

David grasped her hand under the table, and Eden relished the warm, reassuring contact. She knew he was as tense as she was, but he was a master at getting people to talk, and Bertha and Mac recounted with glee their summer excursion into Montana and the Dakotas.

How Beth was holding up was a bigger worry. Eden glanced at her sister. Finding the rose had obviously shaken her; she was shredding her napkin into teeny puffs of paper, and her complexion seemed more sallow than normal. The small portion of cinnamon roll Eden had managed to swallow felt like a glob of petrified dough in her stomach. She had yet to tell Beth about Valerie. The kid was already trembling. Was she strong enough for all this stress?

The telephone rang. Eden jumped as if she'd sat on a tack. So much for her own nerves. Was the caller Rose Hatcher again?

But David handed the phone to Mac, stating that it was his doctor's office calling to confirm the appointment he'd set up. Mac and Bertha excused themselves and went back out to the motor home.

The next second, questions popped from Beth like tennis balls from an electronic server. "Where are we going to go now?"

"I don't know, sweetie." Eden gave Beth's hands a reassuring squeeze.

"We can't stay here." Beth's voice rose an octave. "She'll come back. She'll kill you."

"We'll be long gone before she has the chance." David scooted out of his chair. "The best thing we can do now is let the McFaddens have the house back today. I'll make a few calls and arrange a new hiding place."

He took the cellular phone into the living room, and soon—although they could not make out the words— they heard the soft modulation of his soothing tones.

Beth started to stand. Eden reached a hand toward her. "Sit with me a minute longer, Beth."

She waited until Beth was resettled, then drew a bracing breath. "Yesterday, when David and I went to the Issaquah PD...well...we didn't tell you the entire truth."

Alarm filled Beth's eyes. "Is this more bad news?"

"I'm afraid it is, sweetie."

"What? Are they going to arrest you again?"

"It's not about me." Eden tugged at the back edge of her hair. "It's Val, sweetie."

"What?" The word was impatient. "Just tell me."

"She's dead."

Beth looked as stunned as a rabbit cornered by a pack of hungry coyotes. "How?"

Eden swallowed. "M-murdered."

Beth gasped and tears sprang into her eyes.

"Kollecki told us she'd been stabbed."

"But . . . why?"

"David and I are guessing that the stalker feared she might be able to identify her."

"Why didn't you tell me this last night?"

"After the scare you'd been through?"

"It seems I had good cause to be afraid. Even more than I realized. But I'm not a child, Eden. My life is in as much jeopardy as yours. Quit keeping me in the dark."

Eden wasn't sure she could make such a promise, not if it meant sparing Beth more pain. She said nothing, watching Beth's face crumple in sorrow.

"Poor, jealous old Val. She only wanted to be loved for herself." Tears streamed down Beth's cheeks, and she scrambled from the room. Her footsteps clattered up the staircase.

Eden's heart ached for her, but she didn't go after her. Beth needed to grieve on her own, in her own way. She cleared the table. Her gaze drifted over the lake as she absently washed the dishes, fretting over the meaning of this latest rose, wondering if David had found them a new hideout.

DAVID COULDN'T GET the rose off his mind. Had the stalker killed again? He dialed the Issaquah PD, got Kollecki on the line and told him about the rose.

"Not another one, Doc." Kollecki's voice echoed down the line like a high-pitched, annoying buzz.

"But people unrelated to the case discovered it."

"I don't care if a hundred people witnessed the finding of the damned thing. Find me one person who saw it placed there—other than yourself and Mrs. Prescott, that is—and you'll catch my attention."

"By then it may be too late," David growled, and slammed the Disconnect button before realizing he hadn't told the cop they'd be leaving the area today.

Eden was putting the last dish away as he came into the room. She smiled at him, and his insides warmed, his tension ebbing marginally. He said, "I heard Beth sobbing. You told her?"

Eden nodded. "Did you have any luck?"

"Great luck. A friend of mine has a cabin in a remote area of eastern Washington. He keeps the key hidden outside, so all we have to do is pack and take off."

"Terrific." Eden folded the dish towel, then stood on tiptoe and kissed his cheek. He pulled her closer, folding her to him and kissed her properly. She came away breathless. "We'd better save that for later."

"You ever made love in a rustic cabin?"

She gave him a mischievous laugh. "Before you, I never made love anywhere but in a bed."

"Then, for as long as we're together, we'll avoid a bed whenever possible."

As long as they were together? Nothing mentioned about forever. Hurt pricked Eden's heart. Nothing more permanent than this day-to-day existence. Was that the stalker's fault? Or had she misjudged the depth of David's love for her? She moved out of his arms. She'd be damned if she'd tell him about the baby until she was certain how he felt. She wouldn't use the fact that she might be pregnant with his child to trap any man into a commitment.

"I'll tell Beth," she said. "The sooner we're away from here the better."

David nodded. "And I'll let the McFaddens know they can move back in when they return from the doctor's."

An hour later they were headed up I-90 toward Snoqualmie Pass in Eden's minivan. Beth sat in the rear seat monitoring the three and four lanes of traffic behind them.

Knowing that there was nothing she could do to ease her sister's anxiety, Eden tried easing her own by concentrating on the passing hillsides, the breathtaking array of golden, green, and orange-red leaves, the occasional waterfall and the high, jagged rock formations. The day held the lingering fragrance of summer, but she detected a promise of autumn spicing the air. It was her favorite time of year in the Northwest, a season best spent with good friends and loving family at some wonderful place...like a remote cabin in the mountains...enjoying wholesome activities.

Not running from a killer.

The thought stole what little enjoyment she'd culled from the day. She hunched down in the seat, her gaze scouring the large side mirror as, like Beth, she kept her own vigil on the constantly shifting traffic. A tight knot of frustration pained her chest. How long could they keep running from this woman? How long before they couldn't take it anymore?

How long? Were they supposed to walk away from their former lives forever? Would David be forced to miss the opening week of fall classes at the university? What would happen to his career if this went on indefinitely?

She rolled her tense neck, knowing as surely as the tires clacked on the concrete pavement that *indefinitely* would never come to pass; one or all of them would break before that time. Then what?

"David, did you clear our leaving the county with Kollecki?" she asked.

David's gaze flicked from mirror to windshield to mirror, scanning the vehicles on all sides of them, his eyes peeled for a black compact. "I meant to, but the obnoxious guy ticked me off and I hung up without mentioning it."

"Hadn't we better take care of that now?"

"We'll call him from the cabin."

"Knowing Kollecki, he'll order us right back."

"Well, we aren't going back," David stated firmly. "But you can call him now if it will make you feel better."

They rounded the corner, and Snoqualmie Summit came into view, the ski lifts idle, the grassy mountainsides snowless. Three months would change that. She reached for the telephone. A loud beeping startled her, and she frowned at the cell phone. But the sound wasn't coming from it. "What is that?"

"Probably my beeper," David said, wondering where he'd put it.

"It's *my* beeper." Beth's voice was a falsetto squeak. Eden spun around. "*Your* beeper!"

Beth's eyes were the size of silver dollars, and her hand trembled as she tugged the beeper from her jacket pocket.

David eased the van into the outside lane. Silence vibrated around them as Beth read the message. Finally she looked up at Eden. "It's the hospital."

"We knew that," David said, pulling onto the shoulder of the road. He and Eden exchanged glances. There was no way they could escape to the remote cabin now, but this was the best news Beth could have. He flipped on his blinker. "A U-turn isn't legal, but I'll risk the ticket for you, kiddo."

He waited for a break in traffic, then maneuvered into the westbound lanes. Eden reached back and squeezed Beth's knee. Beth looked as she had the day Peter and Eden married and it appeared they'd belong to a close family again, as they had when Mom and Dad were alive; she looked hopeful yet afraid to hope. "You'd better call Dr. Ingalls."

The telephone conversation confirmed that there was indeed a donor kidney for Beth. Eden beamed at her sister, but Beth wrung her hands in her lap. "What if this one isn't a match, either?"

"Oh, no, you don't. Sometimes good things happen to good people. And we are all going to hang on to positive thoughts, you hear me?"

"Positive thoughts?" She laughed bitterly. "What about the stalker? What if she finds out and comes to the hospital?"

David's gaze met Beth's in the rearview mirror. "We'll see to it that security keeps a close watch on you at all times."

"If the hospital can't promise us that, we'll provide private protection," Eden reassured her. "The only thing you're to worry about is getting well."

"I'm not worried about me. The stalker has no reason to fear me. It's David and you who need the protection."

Eden's joy over the possible kidney for Beth dimmed. A double-edged razor of fear cut through her. Beth's operation was a serious one that might not work, and she was right—by abandoning their plans to hide out, they were walking into God knew what jeopardy.

But maybe that was for the best. Hiding wouldn't draw the woman out of the shadows. Maybe this would force her hand, and they could put an end to her tyranny.

The Emergency room was as deserted as a mall at midnight. The same jolly nurse who had admitted Beth the day of Eden's release from prison was behind the desk. She greeted Beth and David with a toothy smile, her clown's-cap hairdo bobbing. Her greeting to Eden was less cordial, her attitude bordering on rudeness.

So, Eden thought, *she's finally figured out why I looked so familiar.* Her memory was probably jarred by the media coverage surrounding Valerie's death. Although Eden hadn't seen any newspaper or television reports on the murder, she was sure speculation had dragged her name, and her photograph, back into the limelight.

Well, she didn't care a whit how this woman treated her . . . as long as she was kind to Beth. But Beth didn't miss the disdain in the nurse's eyes. She mouthed "I'm sorry" to Eden, then insisted David and she meet her on the fourth floor later.

"She's in good hands," David assured Eden when they were down the hall walking away from Emergency.

"I know, but I still want security alerted."

"So do I. I'll call from my office." He checked his watch. "If we hurry, we'll catch the head of security before he leaves for lunch."

IN DAVID'S OFFICE, Lynzy was making coffee. She didn't bother glancing around. "It's about time you showed up. I was starting to think you'd been in an accident or some—'' She broke off as she turned toward them and crooked her hair behind her left ear. Her brown eyes widened in surprise. "Ms. Prescott. Dr. Coulter. I thought you were Colleen."

David frowned, his gaze sweeping his secretary's desk. The typewriter was still covered, the computer screen black. "You haven't heard from her?"

Eden crossed to the coffee machine and helped herself to a cup.

"No, and that's just not Colleen." Lynzy strode to her desk and set her mug beside a pile of papers she'd apparently been working on before they came in. "She's so particular about details."

"She wasn't expecting me today." David shrugged. "Maybe she's playing hooky."

"That sounds more like me than Colleen. She prides herself on job attendance."

Lynzy was right. Where the hell was Colleen? The image of the white rose they'd found this morning jammed to the front of his brain, and his stomach did a nosedive. "Have you tried calling her at home?"

"Half the morning. But all I get is her machine. I left a couple of messages." She sat down and reached for her mug. "Say, what are you two doing here today anyway?" She paused, and her face brightened. "Tell me you're going to be here next week after all, Doc."

The expectation in her voice reminded David how difficult Dr. Kenneth Levy could be to work with. Lynzy took her job seriously, but she had an irrepressible sense that it should also be pleasant. Pleasant wasn't Dr. Levy's long suit. But Kenneth had been the only one of his colleagues with ten free days to spare. He shook his head at Lynzy. "I'm afraid I'm still on leave."

"Beth is here for a kidney." Eden set her coffee aside, untasted. Was David thinking what she was thinking? That the white rose they'd been left this morning meant Colleen was the stalker's latest victim?

Lynzy let out a disappointed sigh, then blushed. "Oh, don't get me wrong, Ms. Prescott. I'll keep my fingers crossed for your sister, but this means I'm stuck with Dr. Levy for ten more days."

Eden gave her a sympathetic smile, but her insides clamored to get David alone. "Don't we have a telephone call to see to?"

They excused themselves and went into David's office.

The second he closed the door, she said, "Where do you think Colleen is?"

"I'm afraid to guess." His face was ashen. "Let me take care of calling security, then I'll deal with finding her."

He lifted the receiver and poked in the number. A man with an East Indian accent answered, "Security."

David identified himself and asked to speak to the head of security.

"So sorry, Dr. Coulter. He leaves for lunch five minutes past."

"When will he be back?"

"I am expecting him at one-thirty. Perhaps could I be of assist?"

David outlined his problem. The man said, "I see. I have not the authorize for this, but I make the note and my boss he be calling you back when after he returns, please."

"Yes, please." David thanked the man, gave him his pager number and hung up. He turned to Eden. Worry etched her beautiful blue eyes, and he strove to reassure her. "It shouldn't be a problem. But he can't authorize the watch. I should have called from the Emergency desk, but I didn't want any more gossip circulating about this than necessary."

"It's all right. I'm sure Beth will be okay until the man is back from lunch. She'll be under constant scrutiny, and besides, like she said, the stalker has nothing against her. It's you and I who need to be cautious."

"And Colleen?"

"David, there's nothing we can do for Beth for several hours. Would you feel better if we went to Colleen's house and made sure she isn't ... is ... alive and well?"

"You're sure you wouldn't mind?"

"Positive. In fact, I'd feel better myself."

"I'll try ringing her at home first." He looked up her phone number and dialed. After four rings, Colleen's recorded voice asked him to leave a message. He implored her to pick up the phone if she was there. The request was ignored. With a heavy heart, he set the receiver in the cradle. He started around his desk. "She lives in west Seattle."

Lynzy glanced up as they emerged from his office. David said, "We're going to take a drive over to Colleen's. If she should call or show up before I check in again, you can reach me on my cell phone."

A sudden wariness came into her eyes. "You don't think she's been—"

"I have no reason to believe there's any problem," David lied. "And you shouldn't let your fertile imagination run away with any such notions. I'm only checking on Colleen because—as you pointed out—this is unusual behavior for her." He nodded at Eden. "Ready?"

As he reached for the doorknob, it was already spinning. Eden and David stepped back, and the door swung inward. A breathless, rumpled Colleen stood there. She reared back in surprise. The tight knot in David's stomach dissolved in relief.

Colleen and David spoke each other's name in unison. Then he said, "Where have you been? You had us all worried."

She came fully into the room and gestured with her hand that she needed to catch her breath. She moved to her desk, giving him time to assess her appearance. Wisps of her fawn brown hair poked from her French braid like snags on a ratty sweater, and beneath her large blue eyes the skin had a bruised hue as if she hadn't slept in days. Her makeup, usually undetectable, was smudged. Her cheeks were crimson, but he knew that could be from whatever exertion had left her breathless.

Lynzy said, "Why didn't you call? I've been imagining all sorts of horrors."

Colleen's cheeks grew redder, and she lifted her shoulders defensively. "I—I didn't think anyone would be here to take the call. Dr. Coulter was on leave, and you're working with Dr. Levy."

"Never mind that, Colleen." David's voice was as soothing as balm. "Where have you been?"

"In Renton. The nursing home called me about seven last night."

"Colleen's mother has been in a nursing home since she suffered a stroke last winter," David explained to Eden.

Eden nodded and Colleen continued. "She suffered another last night, a severe one. They rushed her to the hospital. That's where I've been. At Valley General. All night."

David, Lynzy and Eden each offered Colleen sympathy. Colleen thanked them and drew a sad, ragged breath. "She's doing as well as can be expected, but she's seventy-five...."

David patted her shoulder. "You didn't need to come in today."

"I know, but I didn't want to be alone. I thought I'd get a book I left in my desk and eat in the cafeteria."

David had never seen his secretary so shaken. "Forget the book. I could use some lunch, too. How about it, Eden? We can't see Beth for a couple more hours. Are you hungry?"

Eden realized what he was doing, and she loved him for it. But to her surprise, she also realized she was famished. It had to be after noon. "That's a great idea."

"Lynzy? I'm buying."

"Dr. Levy? Or a free lunch? Hmm." Lynzy leapt up. "I'm starving."

On the way to the cafeteria, Colleen and Eden commiserated over their mother and sister respectively. Eden realized she faced hope today, while Colleen faced despair, and she counted her blessings. She had David and her sister...and her baby to share the bad times and the good times. When Colleen's mom died, she'd be all alone.

The cafeteria was a hive of buzzing chatter, personnel and visitors eating, talking, coming and going. As they grabbed their trays and joined the food line, Eden noticed a couple of women, strangers, glance at her, then duck their heads together. Obviously more media watchers, she decided, lifting her chin and ignoring them. She was innocent and she damned well wouldn't act otherwise.

David paid for their food and began weaving his way through the crowded tables to a place near the back wall. Colleen was right behind him, trailed by Lynzy. Eden was last in their little procession. As she followed, she felt more eyes on her, but she kept her gaze focused on David and the table he'd chosen.

A white object rested on the tabletop. Her heart stopped. Someone rammed against her. Eden let out a startled gasp, nearly dropping her tray.

"Sorry," the grungy teenage boy murmured, momentarily blocking her view of the table.

Eden stood frozen, unable to respond, unable to move. Please, God, not another rose.

"Whatever," the teenage boy said in exasperation, then shouldered past her.

She could still feel eyes on her and realized she was blocking the narrow space between tables, making a spectacle of herself. She pushed ahead and plunked her tray down opposite David's. Where had the object gone?

"Ms. Prescott? Eden?"

Recognizing Ariel Bell's voice, Eden jerked around. She was seated at the next table with Denise Smalley. Denise's face was set in a serene expression, neither friendly nor hostile.

Eden ignored her. "Hello, Ariel."

"Denise tells me Beth is here for her kidney. Please tell her I'm delighted for her."

"I will. Thank you."

Eden turned back to the table and sat down. Next to Colleen's tray was the object she'd thought was a rose. She almost laughed. It was only a white napkin someone had twisted into a shape that resembled the hated flower.

THE WOMAN TWISTED on her cafeteria chair. Eden and David had thought they could run from her, but there was nowhere for them to hide. Didn't they know that by now?

She ate her salad in silence, wincing inwardly every time she saw Eden bestow a tender gaze on David. *My David!* The scream resounded inside her head, echoing off her pounding temples and blistering the blood that boiled through her veins.

Temper, temper. She could hear her mother's words whispering through the anger fogging her brain. The woman took another bite of salad, chewing thoughtfully. Was that witch Eden pregnant? Had she told David the child was his?

Pain jabbed her heart, refueled her fury. But her expression remained placid, fixed. It was a technique she'd taught herself at the age of eight. As long as she controlled her expressions, Mommy and Daddy couldn't see her emotions, couldn't tell when she was scared or angry, wouldn't beat her worse.

Her gaze stole surreptitiously to David. *You are running out of time, my beloved. Choose me and you choose life. Choose Eden and you choose death.*

Chapter Thirteen

Leaving David in the waiting area, Eden strode down the transplant wing to the room assigned to Beth. A security guard stood outside. In deference to David, the head of security had agreed to lend one of his guards to watch Beth's room until they knew whether or not she'd be staying for surgery. After that, they'd have to hire outside protection.

Eden greeted the guard, donned an isolation mask and entered the fourth-floor room. The bed was empty, but she could hear the shower running, and the sour scent of antiseptic wafted on the steam.

The window shades were drawn against the sun, and as the door closed behind her, she was pitched into near-darkness for two seconds. As her eyes adjusted to the change in light, she realized there was a nurse in the room.

"This *is* Beth Montgomery's room?"

"Yes." The nurse's voice was muffled by her mask, but a shock ran the length of Eden as she recognized the crew-cut, frosted hair and coolly assessing sky blue eyes.

Denise Smalley.

Eden stepped closer. "What are you doing here?"

"Readying your sister's intravenous setup."

A sliver of fear snaked through Eden. Would this woman harm Beth? She took a step closer. "Under the circumstances, don't you think it would be better to remove yourself from Beth's case?"

"If you have a problem with my being here, you may ask to have me removed." Denise was as wooden as a tongue depressor. "But I assure you, I'll take better care of your sister than you did of mine."

Eden blanched. "I had nothing to do with your sister's death."

"You got off on a technicality." Although she hadn't said it, the tone of Denise's statement held a save-it-for-someone-who-believes-you quality. "That's not the same as being innocent."

Innocence was such a fragile thing, Eden mused, taking a deep breath. More than half of the Northwest believed *she* was guilty of double murder, but at this moment it was only Denise's opinion that mattered...and how it could affect Beth. "I—I didn't even know your sister."

"That makes it all the worse." Denise sighed. "She was a great kid, and I miss her every minute of every day. Do you understand that? Do you know how painful it will be for you if this kidney isn't a match for Beth and the right one can't be found in time?"

Oh, dear God, yes. Eden had lived with the fear of that outcome for the past year. "I've had to face the possibility of losing Beth."

"You're luckier than I in that regard. One day Shannon was healthy, so excited about her life, the next she was gone. Snatched from me like that." She snapped her fingers, but the rubber gloves she wore reduced the snap to a snick. "I loved her so much. And like some insidious cancer, it eats at me every day, because it wasn't fair and because I had no chance to preadjust to the loss.''

The heartache in Denise's voice both frightened and confused Eden; she sympathized with the loss of her sister, but the murder of a loved one often roused the need for retaliation in grieving relatives. And if Denise was the woman obsessed with David, she was already over the edge. She watched Denise finish with the IV and walk to the bed. Could Eden risk placing Beth in her care?

Her stomach was knotted, and her palms felt damp. It struck her that she was branding this woman guilty without more than circumstantial evidence—exactly as she'd been branded by the police and the press. Her gaze swept over the IV bag, innocently hanging from its metal post. Would a nurse risk poisoning a patient when she would be the first one suspected? No. Denise was not stupid. Besides, would a woman who loved her sister as much as she professed to have loved Shannon be able to take a gun and shoot her?

Eden couldn't imagine it was possible, and she suspected David and she would soon erase Denise's name from their suspect list. But that didn't mean Beth should be left in her care.

Denise folded the covers back from the bed. "I understand Beth is all the blood family you have left.''

"Yes." Her stomach gave another anxious twinge. What would happen if she had Dr. Ingalls remove Denise from this case? Would she seek revenge? Eden decided this topic would best be discussed with David. The sooner the better.

"Then her death would be doubly hard on you. Oh, don't look so distressed. I wouldn't wish that on anyone. Not even—''

The unspoken "you" hung between them as the bathroom door clicked open, emitting the steamy antiseptic scent into the room and grabbing their attention. Eden stepped to one side, allowing Denise, who was more sterile, to assist Beth in fastening her gown.

Forgetting that the mask hid most of her face, Eden smiled at her sister. "How are you holding up, sweetie?"

"I'm tired."

"Of course you are." Denise helped her into bed. "But as soon as I start the IV, you can rest."

Beth's rest was interrupted almost immediately by the arrival of the first in a series of doctors who would re-examine her. Eden promised she'd return in a while and left. Denise followed her into the hall. "Are you going to have me removed from this case?"

Eden wasn't sure what she was going to do yet. She said noncommittally, "I'm certain you'll handle Beth as you'd wish someone would handle Shannon if she was in this same situation."

Her pugnacious stance eased marginally. "We should be hearing soon . . . about the cross-match."

With that, Denise turned on her heel and headed down the hall, disappearing into a supply room.

Eden returned to the waiting area. David and Ariel occupied adjoining chairs and were chatting softly. They glanced up as she approached, but it was David who stole her attention. His gaze projected concern that she knew was as much for her well-being as for Beth's. A rush of warmth swirled around her heart, and she longed to fold herself into his arms, to feel his heat and his love soaking through her, and to let them wash away her distress. She glanced self-consciously at Ariel and pasted on a smile.

David rose. "Any news yet?"

"No." She gestured for him to sit, then she took the chair opposite. "Denise says we should be hearing soon."

"Denise?" His brows crumpled, and she could see he was having the same concern she'd had initially. She ached to talk to him about it.

"Denise is Beth's case nurse?" Ariel's gray eyes widened beneath her fringe of sandy bangs. "Is that a good idea? Feeling as she does about..." Pink colored her cheeks. "I mean, surely it's no secret how she feels about you, Eden?"

"No. It's no secret." In fact, Eden didn't doubt Ariel had heard an earful about it at lunch earlier. The thought of Denise at the IV packet bounced into her mind. She had done the right thing, hadn't she—letting Denise attach the needle to Beth's vein? "We had a talk about sisters, and I got the impression she'd give Beth the kind of care she'd have wanted for Shannon."

Ariel leaned forward, her hot-pink top straining against her ample bosom. "What exactly did she say about Shannon?"

Wariness swayed through Eden. "Only that she loved her and missed her every day."

Ariel sat back, her bangs lowering over her eyes as she arched her brows. "I expect she misses the competition."

"Competition?" Eden glanced at David. His lips were pressed in a flat line, and she had the distinct impression he knew where this was leading. "What kind of competition?"

"The usual. Sisters *will* fall for the same men...." Ariel shook her head. "I think it's an eleventh commandment or something."

Eden could not fathom the implication. "Are you saying Denise was in love with Peter?"

"No, not Peter. Denise never mentioned him. She thought Shannon was interested in...someone else. I don't think she knew about Peter before the murders."

"She claims she did," David interjected.

"Does she? Huh." Ariel shrugged. "I was positive she didn't know about him. In fact, if Shannon was seriously considering marriage, I can't imagine her risking Denise's predatory nature."

Eden grimaced. Although Shannon Smalley had fit Peter's criteria for this year's "trophy wife," Denise with her boyish figure and crew-cut hairstyle did not. That didn't mean she couldn't have seduced him for a casual roll in the hay. "Just how predatory is her nature?"

"She'd put a lioness to shame. Shannon and she competed for boys like opposing schools pursuing a state championship all during their teenage years and after. Denise claims she won more often than she lost, but honestly...Shannon had all the looks, and the sweet disposition. It's like the old saying, blood tells."

David remained silent, but Eden could see he'd heard this all before and wasn't going to gossip about a deceased friend. She wasn't bound by that ethic; she hadn't known Shannon. "Blood tells what?"

"Blood. Relatives. You knew they weren't blood sisters, didn't you?"

David nodded, but Eden shook her head. Renewed worry for Beth clawed her stomach. "Stepsisters?"

"Yes. Shannon's mom came from some fine old family out of Boston. When she divorced her first husband, the fine old bunch of them yanked the silver spoon out of her mouth, then permanently grabbed up the rest of the flatware when she married Denise's widowed father, a hard-drinking dockworker."

The image of Denise extolling love for her sister and talking about the importance of blood relatives ripped across Eden's mind. It had been a lie to put her at ease, to keep her from getting Denise dismissed from Beth's case.

Something dark and ugly slithered through her chest. She leapt to her feet, her gaze locked with David's. "Denise was in Beth's room when I arrived. She was doing something to the IV—"

She couldn't say it, couldn't put her fear into words. Fortunately he understood and stood immediately. "You can't suspect she'd do anything to the saline solution?"

"Hey, Denise is a good nurse." Ariel, also abandoning her chair, sounded offended. Apparently it was all right for her to bad-mouth her friend, but not for them to do it.

"Three murders have been committed," Eden reminded them, struggling to keep the hysteria from her voice. "The police are no closer to solving any of them than the day Shannon and Peter died. We cannot afford to take unnecessary risks."

Ariel's hands were on her hips, her face red with outrage. "Denise did not kill her sister!"

"No one's saying she did," David offered in a lowered voice.

"Maybe not, but Ariel has to admit she just supplied Denise with motive." Eden didn't know if she was more afraid that Denise was a murderer or a revenge-seeking victim.

"Well, I—" Ariel blanched. "Look, how can I help prove she's innocent?"

"What's important right now is getting that IV she gave Beth changed." Eden struggled against the panic nipping her nerves.

David's eyes were rounded. "Denise wouldn't poison one of her patients."

"It's doubtful, I agree. But I'm not willing to risk Beth's life in case I'm wrong. Are you?"

He considered, his face turning into an unreadable mask. It was likely he was recalling the rose they'd found that morning, recalling that they still weren't certain why it had been left. "I'll find Dr. Ingalls and arrange for a change of nurses."

"Thank you." Eden gave him a loving smile. "I'll meet you in Beth's room."

He headed into the hall ahead of her. Ariel called out Eden's name.

Anxious to get to Beth, she turned an impatient, questioning glance at the woman.

Ariel said, "If you don't mind, I'll stick around for a while. If Beth is going to have surgery, I'd like the chance to wish her well. You see, I'm starting a new case tomorrow—on Bainbridge Island, a little girl in a body cast—and I don't expect I'll get back to Seattle for a couple of months."

"I don't mind." Eden only wanted to get to Beth, but she softened her expression. "As soon as we hear something, I'll let you know."

Eden hurried into the transplant corridor. Striding toward her was Denise Smalley, her face as dark as a thundercloud. She glared at Eden. "I will pay you back for all the pain you've brought on me."

"Denise?" Ariel, apparently hearing her friend's raised voice, had wasted no time reaching the two women. "You don't want to make the situation worse."

She started to touch her friend's arm. Denise snatched her arm out of reach. "She had me pulled off this case. The situation couldn't get any worse than that...unless this witch accused me of tampering with the saline solution."

A guilty flush scurried into Eden's face. She held her breath, hoping Ariel would have the good sense not to confirm this—at least until Denise was calmer.

But Denise read the guilt she couldn't hide.

"You did, didn't you?" Outraged, she poked a finger against Eden's chest. "I don't get mad, lady. I get even," Denise warned between clenched teeth. Then she spun away.

Ariel shrugged apologetically at Eden, then hurried after her friend. Eden drew a steadying breath and turned toward Beth's room again. She'd weathered worse storms than Hurricane Denise, but the woman's threat followed her into Beth's room, sweeping into the darkened space and swirling through the shadows.

Eden's breath struggled against the isolation mask.

Her eyes were slow to adjust to the change in light, but finally she saw Beth clearly. Her body was still. Too still? Her eyes were closed, and her face had the peaceful expression of...a corpse. Eden's heart stumbled, and she gasped out, "Beth?"

Beth's eyelids fluttered open. "What? Eden, is that you?"

Relief flushed through Eden, but her voice jammed in her throat.

Beth let out a loud sigh. "Is there any word yet?"

"Nope." Recovering control of her emotions, Eden moved to the bed, still not convinced that Beth had suffered no ill effects from the contents of the IV bag. "How are you feeling?"

Beth grimaced. "What do you think?"

The door swung inward, and a nurse entered, carrying a new intravenous bag. She said hello, then set to work exchanging the saline packets.

Beth frowned. "What are you doing?"

"Nothing to fret over." The nurse's eyes crinkled. "This one just isn't dripping fast enough."

Eden followed the nurse out of the room and found David and Dr. Ingalls waiting in the hallway. Dr. Ingalls said, "Take that directly down to the lab. Felix is expecting it."

"What about Beth's surgery?" Eden reached for David's hand, glad for the warmth that flowed up her arm as his fingers laced with hers.

"If that IV bag hasn't been tampered with—" Dr. Ingalls gave her one of his rare smiles "—we'll be giving your sister a new kidney tonight."

Eden wanted to shout with joy. She settled for hugging David. But the unsettling sensation of being watched made her pull away. At the end of the hall, she spotted Denise Smalley. Her eyes were narrowed, shooting daggers of hatred directly at Eden. Frissons of ice spiked down Eden's spine.

"It was saline solution," Dr. Ingalls informed them an hour later.

In that place inside her where she held all the unfairness of being wrongly accused, Eden despised herself for accusing Denise Smalley just as unfairly. But the truth was, Beth's life had to be considered above anyone's hurt feelings. "Let's tell Beth."

The look of joy and relief on Beth's face matched the happiness dancing inside Eden. The next minutes passed in a swirl of activity and doctors. As Beth was finally wheeled into surgery, David caught Eden's arm.

She glanced up at him, suddenly weary to the bone. But she was too keyed up for sleep. David conjured a deck of cards, and they played Hearts, which he excelled at, and Crazy Eights, which she couldn't lose. Between games, they walked the corridor, stretching their limbs, burning off pent-up nerves, drinking coffee, reagitating those same nerves and silently praying... for Beth's well-being, for Dr. Ingalls's expertise and for the grieving family of the kidney donor.

After what seemed an eternity, Eden asked, "How long has it been?"

"Not long enough, love. But I can think of a wonderful way to make the next hour pass in sublime pleasure." His eyes were the color of a mossy glade, and she knew she could get lost in them, fall willingly into his arms and let him take her to the paradise he offered.

"You have no idea how tempting that sounds." She reached up to touch his face. He needed a shave, but it did nothing to mar her attraction to him. A tingling heat swished through her.

"Hey, Doc." Lynzy's voice startled Eden.

She jerked her hand away from David's face, reining in the sweet feelings he roused in her.

Lynzy projected an energy force that was tangible, overpowering Eden's waning strength and making her more aware than ever of how strung out she felt. Lynzy flipped her long brown hair, her eyes sparkling like boiling coffee. "I called the transplant wing. They told me the great news."

David smiled at her, his eyes teasing. "Finished with Dr. Levy for the day?"

"No. But I was looking for you, Doc. Two things. First, the security guard you hired arrived, and I directed him to Transplant to wait for Beth's arrival."

"Great." David nodded.

"Thank you," Eden added.

"Second," Lynzy said, "some woman keeps calling and hanging up when I ask her name. The last time, I told her to call back in half an hour and I'd make sure you were there. It's almost that time now."

Foreboding pricked Eden.

David's smile faded. "You didn't recognize the voice?"

"I didn't think about it, but now that you mention it, maybe." She waved her hand in frustration. "Oh, I don't know. It sounded kind of muffled...like she had a cold or spoke with a nasal twang."

David shook his head, then gazed at Eden. "You coming or staying?"

As much as she hated leaving the surgery waiting room, she was not about to stay there alone. "Coming." They arrived in his office with minutes to spare. But the phone remained silent past the deadline. Five minutes. Ten minutes. Fifteen minutes. David's patience snapped. "This is ridiculous. Let's go back. If the woman calls again, Lynzy, transfer her directly to my message center."

Eden and he headed for the door. The telephone rang, its peal as jarringly loud in the office as an alarm bell. David let it ring twice before snatching up the receiver on Colleen's desk. "Dr. Coulter."

Eden felt as if she were still trying to breathe through the isolation mask.

"Oh, Dr. Coulter, I was afraid I'd never reach you." It was Rose Hatcher.

He mouthed the name to Eden. Her heart hitched.

A pulse beat in his throat, and David strove to keep his excitement and concern out of his voice. "What do you want?"

"I need to see you, Dr. Coulter. Please, say you'll help me."

"How can I, Rose? You say you didn't kill Marianne, but I can't prove it. Can you?"

There was a lengthy pause. "Then you won't help me?"

"I don't see how I can. I don't know who killed Marianne."

"But I do. Now."

"What?" His pulse wobbled. "Who?"

"No. Not over the phone. How do I know she's not there with you now?"

He glanced at Eden and Lynzy, frowning. "This is absurd. If you don't tell me, I'll hang up."

"If you want to know, meet me at your house tonight. At midnight. I'll be watching...so don't bring the police."

David opened his mouth to respond, then realized he was listening to a dead line. She'd hung up.

Chapter Fourteen

David replaced the receiver in its cradle with a jerky motion. His face felt hot, his body cold. Did Rose really know who the murderer was? Or was this just another ploy to make him think *she* wasn't the murderer?

Eden touched his arm.

He flinched as if she'd stung him.

Frowning, Eden stepped back. "What did Rose say?"

"That was Rose Hatcher?" Lynzy looked stunned . . . and a bit afraid.

David nodded but ignored Eden's question. His mind was racing. Rose had suggested the murderer could be here with him. He couldn't tell them that. Nor did he believe it. Eden was not a killer, and Lynzy . . . she was so candid, the thought was ludicrous.

Granted, people often presented deceptive facades to the world, guarding their true selves—the reasons they did so were as vast and complex as the human population. And, contrarily, those who had the most-obvious neuroses—like straitlaced Colleen—were usually much healthier than one imagined.

An ache started at his temples. Was Lynzy hiding her true self from the world, or was she what she appeared to be? She *was* on their suspect list, and without some solid proof, he couldn't just rule her out. But, so help him, he couldn't believe it of her.

"David, what's wrong?" Eden intruded on his troubled musing. "What did she say?"

Watching Lynzy for a telltale reaction, he said, "Rose claims to know who the murderer is."

Lynzy's big brown eyes rounded. "I don't understand. Isn't *she* the murderer?"

The innocence of the question was just what he'd wanted to hear from Lynzy. The knot in his stomach loosened.

Eden's stomach clenched. She drew in a shallow breath. "Did Rose tell you who she thinks is guilty?"

"No." He decided against mentioning Rose's wanting to meet him later that night. Eden would have a fit, and Lynzy would wonder why he didn't immediately call the police. But somehow his doubts about Rose were causing him to resist that natural next step. "When I asked if she had proof, she hung up. She was probably lying."

Sensing some kind of distraction vibrating from David, Eden deduced that he was the one ducking the truth. A rush of anticipation spurted through her. What had Rose told him that he wasn't sharing? She had to know. Now. "It's getting late. Beth will be out of surgery soon."

"Yeah, we'd better get back." David followed her to the door, then stopped as though something had just occurred to him. "It's almost six, Lynzy. What are you still doing here anyway?"

She pointed to the two neat piles on her desk. "I'm not making as much headway as I'd like. I think I'll work another hour or so."

"See you tomorrow, then." David ushered Eden from his offices.

As soon as they were ten feet down the hallway, Eden pulled up short. "You're holding out on me. What else did Rose have to say?"

David grinned wryly. "Think you know me pretty well, don't you?"

"I guess I am starting to pick up a few signals."

His face grew serious. "Rose said she knows who the killer is. But I had no luck getting a name out of her."

"And...?"

His expression went from serious to grim. "She'll tell me the murderer's name only if I meet her at my house at midnight tonight."

"No." Fear clutched Eden's chest. "You can't do that."

"Don't worry. I'm not going to meet her. Not as long as I'm not positive that she's innocent."

Eden breathed a sigh of relief. "She's probably just trying to separate us."

David ushered her onto the elevator. "Who knows what she's thinking?"

Eden tried not to show how much she wished she knew that very thing. She stepped to the back of the elevator and watched him push the button. "Shouldn't we call the police and tell them that Rose will be at your house around midnight?"

"I'll put a call in to them as soon as we know how Beth is."

"Okay." Her stomach was uneasy. Were they doing the right thing...turning Rose over to the police? What if she was innocent? Her neck muscles felt pinched. All this stress couldn't be good for her. Or for the baby.

With an iron-willed effort, she relegated Rose Hatcher and the stalker to the furthest recesses of her mind. If she had to be stressed about something, it ought be her sister. "I pray the surgery is going right."

IT WAS EIGHT O'CLOCK before Dr. Ingalls appeared in the surgery waiting room. He looked as tired as Eden felt. But his weary features shone with the pleasure of a job well done. "Beth came through like a trooper. The rest is in God's hands. She'll be asleep for hours. Why don't you go home and get some shut-eye yourselves? Come back tomorrow." He started to turn away, then hesitated as if he'd recalled Valerie's murder and the fact that Eden probably wasn't presently staying at home. "Just leave a number where you can be reached ... in case ..."

In case Beth's body rejects the kidney. The unspoken words scuttled through Eden's head like a black cloud. She shook herself and willed the tension in her stomach to ease. Dr. Ingalls had stated the fact. Whether or not Beth's body accepted this kidney was in God's hands; she could do nothing ... except pray for a positive outcome.

"Dr. Ingalls is a wise man," David said. "Let's take a taxi to the Four Seasons and order room service."

"That's the second-best suggestion you've made all day." She gave him a sensuous grin that started his heart zipping merrily against his ribs.

"We'll call from my office."

His office was dark when they entered. The piles on Lynzy's desk looked the same to Eden as when they'd left two hours earlier. "Looks like Lynzy took your advice and went home after all."

"Yeah. I'm kind of surprised she didn't get more done. She's usually a whiz."

David telephoned for a cab, then they returned to the main building of the medical center. Visiting hours had recently ended. They joined the flow of people streaming through the main corridor toward the exits, then held back at the front doors to wait for the cab.

"Hey, it's raining." David spoke softly, but his face shone with surprise as he pointed at the rain lashing the concrete walkway outside.

"When did this storm blow in?" Eden eyed the dark night uneasily, belatedly realizing the drumming noise she heard was coming from the rain hitting the Plexiglas windows of the solarium and the covered walk.

David shrugged. "Probably started while we were at lunch."

Eden felt an ominous gloom hovering nearby. Was it the storm? Or simply being here, near the solarium? The last time she'd been here, someone had left a rose in her purse. The last time she'd been here someone had been watching her.

Without warning, the prickly sensation of eyes drilling her back struck her again. No. She would not look around. Would not give whoever was doing this to her the satisfaction of knowing they'd frightened her.

Instead, she inched closer to David, needing his warmth, his strength.

"It's coming down pretty hard." David draped his arm around her shoulders and pulled her to his side.

Headlights swept through the downpour, and a yellow cab appeared on the tarmac. They dashed through the torrent and hurried to it, arriving wet but safe. Eden wiped the water from her face with her sleeve and snuggled against David, truly comfortable now that they were out of sight of prying eyes.

But once they were in their suite with dinner ordered, she wondered if she should have mentioned her feeling of being watched to David. What if the stalker had followed them here? But David bolted the hotel door, reviving her sense of security.

The invitation was back in his mossy green eyes. "How does a long hot shower sound?"

"Delicious." He hadn't touched her, and she was already breathless, already anticipating his hands on her, already parting her lips to meet his descending mouth.

His hands curled around her upper arms, and he pulled her close, clasping her sensitive breasts against his firm chest. Her nipples sprang taut, achingly responsive to the very brush of his body to hers. His tongue delved into her mouth, rough against smooth, tasting, pleasuring, sending sweet, shattering shards of desire spiking through her, the heat melting her stress, dissolving her tension, liquefying her insides to something thick and hot like bubbling sugar.

What was this need to feel his naked flesh against her own? Had she always had this abandon untapped inside her? Her mind was glazed with want, her ability to reason such issues reduced to so much spun candy.

Why question joy? Eden tugged his shirt hem free from his pants and shoved her hands beneath the soft cotton fabric until she connected with his warm, muscled body. She groaned his name on a breathy sigh.

Then they were tearing at each other's clothes. Her sweater dropped to the floor, then her jeans, his sweatshirt, his jeans, her bra, her panties, his shorts, his socks.

She stood back in awe, her gaze skimming every inch of him from his head to his toes. "You are the most gorgeous man...."

"Gorgeous?" He snagged her wrists, then swept her to him, his grin adding to his heart-stopping looks. "You are the beauty, my love."

"If there's any truth in that—" his need pressed hard and hot against her stomach, and her inner pulse throbbed to have him inside her "—it's that you make me *feel* beautiful."

"Let me reaffirm that for you now." Kissing her, he lifted her into his arms and carried her into the bathroom.

Eden had the vague impression of tile and glass and brass fixtures as golden as the paradise that David wrapped her in.

The shower was large enough for four. Water sprayed from a brass faucet head, spilling down on them like some lush spring on a tropical island. He lathered his hands, then began soaping Eden's body, gently massaging her neck, her shoulders, her breasts.

She threw back her head, her eyes closed to the water spilling across her face, and sighed his name. Her nipples strained against his touch, and she arched into his hands, delighting in the friction of their tender massage.

Then his hands slipped lower, gliding over her belly, and Eden tensed. Would he notice its new roundness? She hated not telling him about the baby. Hated worse not knowing whether or not he was the father. But his words "for as long as we're together" rang inside her head and reinforced her conviction that she would not use this pregnancy to trap him into a commitment.

His hands, doing wild things to her body, his mouth pleasuring her, grabbed her attention and sent her troubled thoughts skittering away. "Oh, David."

She could no longer resist touching him. She reached for the fragrant French milled bar and lathered her hands, then began washing him as he had washed her, spending long minutes enjoying the sensuous play of her palms over his sinewy chest and washboard stomach, his lean, taut buttocks, finally wrapping her fingers around his erection and sliding soap-slicked strokes up and down that hard, fevered flesh.

"Eden," he cried, pulling back with desire-glazed eyes.

Steam swirled around them, floating, rising. Warm water sprayed down over their bodies, sweeping away the soapy suds. His gaze was hungry now, his breath as quick and ragged as her own.

Moving behind her, David cupped her breasts and gently pulled her back to his front, then he slipped inside her. And as small as she was, she took all of him as if God had created her especially for him alone. Need— throbbing, coursing—drove him deeper and faster into those hot, tight, moist depths.

Lost in the fervor of their joining, Eden felt herself spiraling out of control, higher and higher, her breath quicker and quicker, her heartbeat wilder and wilder, until she crested the peak with a shout of triumph that sliced through the foggy steam and echoed off the bathroom walls seconds before David's did the same.

THEY ATE DINNER in robes provided by the hotel, then afterward curled up on the deep-cushioned sofa with cups of coffee. Eden felt as sleepy as a sated cat in a sunny window. The only shadow over her mood was a stray thought about Rose Hatcher. "Did you contact the police?"

"I tried getting hold of Tagg, but he wasn't in. I'll be damned if I'd give Kollecki the information. I wouldn't sic him on anyone, not even Rose."

The shadow gained density. "What if Rose isn't the murderer? Have you thought who else might be?"

"No, but she had me considering Lynzy pretty seriously."

Eden lifted her brows in surprise. "Really? To me, Lynzy seems the least suspicious of all our suspects. She's too obvious to be a liar, let alone a murderer."

"That's just it." David took a swallow from his cup. "In any good mystery novel, the least suspicious person is usually the guilty one."

"This isn't fiction." Eden laughed. "Besides... Lynzy seemed to genuinely think that Rose was the murderer. Do you think she was faking that?"

"No. Then again, I believed with all my heart that Rose had killed Marianne. Now... well, I have to admit, I've had my doubts." He opened his arms, and Eden scooted closer, resting her head against his shoulder. He said, "Okay...for the sake of speculation, let's suppose Rose *is* innocent. Who would you suspect?"

"If not Rose..." Eden didn't even have to think about that. "Denise. If looks could kill, I'd have died on the spot from the one she gave me when she saw me in your arms at the hospital right after she was taken off Beth's case." She craned her neck sideways and gazed up at him. "How do you feel about her—could she have murdered her stepsister?"

He rubbed his chin. "I knew Denise and Shannon carried on a fierce competition over men. But Shannon made it clear to me that she cared too much about Denise to let any man really come between them.''

Did Denise feel that same loyalty? Eden stifled a yawn. "Ariel hinted that, too. But how can we know if Denise felt that way about Shannon?''

"Maybe there is no way to know. Hell, maybe we should wonder about Ariel." David toyed with a strand of Eden's raven hair, short and ragged edged, framing her face and emphasizing the cornflower blue of her eyes. "Ariel seemed eager enough to accuse Denise of sibling jealousy, but what about her own motives?''

"What do you mean?''

"Could she have anything against Shannon, or Valerie, or Peter?''

Eden recalled her suspicion that Ariel had told Kollecki how Peter verbally abused the women of his family. It seemed even more plausible now that she *was* the one who'd told the cop. "She might have resented the way Peter sometimes talked to Beth . . . but would that give her motive?''

"It doesn't seem likely. Could he have done something specific to Ariel? Something we don't know about?''

"Certainly." She curled her feet beneath her. She was quiet for a moment, then it struck her they were looking at this all wrong. "David, since we believe the murderer is a stalker, shouldn't the real issue be how all of these women feel about you?''

She was right. That was the way they should consider all their suspects. But, dammit, it was degrading enough even *thinking* about being the object of someone's demented obsession; trying to imagine one of their suspects as that "someone" made him sick. "I know Ariel was grateful when I recommended her to you. But she'd done a super job nursing James's daughter last summer when Mindy's first attempt at waterskiing resulted in a broken pelvis. And you know how good she's been with Beth. As to her feelings for me...I haven't noticed anything. But I can't say I was looking, either. What do you think?''

"To be honest, I've been so wound up in my own problems, I haven't paid that kind of attention to any of our suspects." But she should have. She grew thoughtful again. "What about Colleen? Secretaries often fall for their bosses."

"She's hard to read. Plus she's been too tied up with her mother to have been at the lake house."

"Has she?" Eden sat straighter. "Aren't we taking her at her word?"

He frowned and swore again. "That's the trouble...we're both so basically honest that we've been taking everyone at their word. Colleen's alibi is something we can check out. I'll call the nursing home in the morning."

Eden settled against his shoulder again, and David shut his eyes, letting his mind roll over his earlier thoughts about neuroses and people like Colleen. Was she an obsessive personality? Lynzy certainly was. Even when she had lots to do, her desk was always tidy, a place for anything and everything....

But Colleen, for all her prissy attire and prim appearance, was slower and, if he were honest, less efficient.

Denise had plenty of obsessive behavior, now that he thought of it. She denied her softer side, keeping her emotions rigidly controlled. Her hair and clothes were, if nothing else, bother free.

Ariel, on the other hand, seemed a free spirit with her tousled hair and her hot-pink nursing outfits. But she was a fanatic about her patients, keeping precise charts and following exacting routines.

Which if any of them had violent tendencies?

He ought to know.

Which if any of them had an obsession with him?

He ought to know that, too.

But he didn't.

RAGE BOILED through the woman's veins. She gripped the letter opener like the dagger it resembled and slashed its blood-crusted tip across the photograph of David's face, cutting a jagged tear from ear to ear.

He had chosen Eden.

Revenge whistled through the hollow pit in her chest where once her loving heart had pulsed. Now that organ was but a shriveled black lump, too dark for a ray of sympathy, too dried-up to provoke tears, too small to ache at his betrayal.

She stabbed the picture again, digging the tip of the letter opener into his temple like a pin poked into a voodoo doll. David had sealed his own fate. He wasn't going to die. But he was going to wish he had.

IN THE QUEEN-SIZE BED of the hotel suite, Eden fell asleep in David's arms. He liked the feel of her nestled against him. She was so tiny and so tough. He smiled to himself, realizing he liked both those things about this woman. His woman. Damn. He also liked the sound of that.

But would she? He blew out a melancholy breath. Eden was recently widowed and, unhappy marriage or not, as abandoned as she was in their lovemaking and as much as she seemed to care for him, he knew better than to entangle himself with someone on the rebound. Yet he had jumped in with both feet. If she broke his heart, it would serve him right.

He kissed the top of her head, inhaling the sweet, fragrant scent of her silky hair. *Would* she break his heart?

Thunder boomed overhead as if God were confirming this fear. He shuddered and shoved the awful thought away. But the rain hitting the window seemed to tap the thought free. Gingerly he disentangled himself so as not to wake Eden, then threw off his covers and strolled into the bathroom.

Whiskers grazed his jaw, and his hair was tousled. The troubled man reflected in the mirror brought to mind another rainy night that he'd stood staring at himself like this.

His gaze fell to the counter, to the complimentary comb provided by the hotel. A sudden shiver scurried down his spine as the thing he'd struggled for days to recall popped clear and whole into his head. Combs. Three combs had been taken from his house two months before Rose Hatcher had escaped from jail.

He let out a pent-up breath. She couldn't have taken them. Nor could she have taken Valerie's gun from her Mercedes. And Valerie would have mentioned seeing Rose driving through her neighborhood. Unless Rose was disguised. But that also ruled her out as the woman Valerie had thought she recognized.

It didn't prove she hadn't killed Marianne, but it meant she was innocent of the more recent murders.

Did she really know who the killer was?

Dear God, was she completely innocent as he'd thought when she'd first been arrested? Eden had told him to trust his gut. He decided to do just that. What time was it?

He hurried back into the bedroom and found his watch. Not quite eleven. If he left right away, he could still keep the rendezvous with her.

He tossed on the clothes he'd left heaped on the floor, scribbled Eden a note and pinned it to his pillow. The note was only a precaution. He doused the lights, confident that Eden would be safe here, that he would be gone and back before she even woke.

Minutes later he exited the elevator into the lobby. His attention was so focused on the coming meeting with Rose Hatcher, he didn't notice the raincoat-clad woman ducking into a corner as he headed for the front doors.

Chapter Fifteen

Eden's dreams were haunted by the stalker. She was at the hospital again, feeling those eyes drilling into her back. This time she looked around and scanned the crowd. There *she* was. Standing in the shadows near the corridor to the Health Sciences Building. Eden turned to tell David.

But he was gone.

Eden spun back to the woman. A man was hurrying toward the shadowy figure. *David. No.* She wanted to snatch him back to the safety of her embrace. He was too far away.

She set out after him, calling his name. He didn't seem to hear. He kept on, racing after the shadowy woman, away from the main corridor into the Health Sciences Building. She saw them duck into a stairwell and followed them down two flights to the basement. Terror ran with Eden, speeding her heart to a breathless tempo.

The basement was a maze of halls, eerily shadowed. David and the woman disappeared through one endless hall, then another and another, each darker than the last. Eden tried to quicken her pace, but her legs were leaden and it seemed to take forever to travel a short distance.

She rounded a corner and stepped into total darkness. She tensed, frozen like a snow sculpture. "David?"

He didn't answer. Where was he? Had the woman done something to him? Eden couldn't breathe at the thought. Where was the woman?

A disembodied laugh rang from the darkness, and a glowing yellow light suddenly filled the end of the hall. The woman was still a shadowy haze, reflected in the queer light. But Eden could see David clearly, and her heart was seized with pain. He lay at the woman's feet, a dagger protruding from his chest.

Horror riveted Eden in place for a full second. She leapt forward, railing at the woman with all her might. As she reached David, she dropped to her knees beside his lifeless body. The eerie light shrank from David and skimmed up the woman's body like a false moon. Despite her fear for David, Eden couldn't resist its powerful lure; she lifted her head and gazed at the woman.

The woman had no face.

Eden jerked awake. Pitch darkness greeted her, momentarily disorienting her. Her body was damp with sweat, her heart pummeled her chest wall. It took long seconds to recall she was in a hotel room. With David. She sagged in relief and began shaking off the nightmare, but as her roaring heart quieted, she realized the only breathing in the room was her own.

She felt across the bed for David. His place was empty. Cold to the touch. She lurched to a sitting position. Had he gone into the bathroom? "David?"

Silence. She called out louder. Still no answer. She switched on the bedside light, blinked against the sudden brightness and scrambled out of the bed. She searched the suite. He was gone. Like in her dream. Her heart thumped unsteadily.

No. She was being macabre. The stalker hadn't gotten David. But his bed was cold. He'd been gone for some time.

Worried and befuddled, she strode back into the bedroom. A slip of white paper was stuck to his pillow. She let out a shuddery breath, snatched it up and read quickly. Her relief scurried away, and the chilling sweat once again flushed her body. Had he lost his mind?

No. She forced herself to calm down and reason out his motives. She sank onto the bed, clutching the note to her heart. He wouldn't have gone to meet Rose unless something had convinced him she was no threat. What? She reread the note. Nothing. Not one little clue.

A noise from the living room startled her. Was it the door? David? She leapt off the bed to investigate. The door locks were still engaged. Disappointment rattled through her. What had she heard? The storm?

She ambled back into the bedroom, catching sight of the note, now crumpled on the floor. Images of her nightmare replayed, and a fear as chilling and harsh as the wind flailing the windows swept through her. David might have come up with some reason to trust Rose Hatcher, but she had no cause to believe the woman wasn't a cold-blooded killer.

What if she meant to kill him?

Eden grabbed the phone and dialed David's number. After the twentieth ring, she hung up. Fear squeezed her chest. She tried calming herself. It wasn't midnight; maybe he hadn't reached the house yet.

Good. She didn't want him meeting Rose alone. She made two more quick calls, then dressed and hurried downstairs to meet the taxi she'd ordered.

THE DOWNPOUR was relentless. The taxi maneuvered cautiously through the water-clogged Seattle streets and onto the freeway. Eden perched uneasily on the back seat. Her sense that something was wrong increased with each mile marker they passed. "Could you go a little faster?"

The cabdriver glanced at her in the rearview mirror. "I'm doing as good as I can for the conditions, lady."

She knew he was. He switched lanes, spewing a jet of water at a taxi parked on the side of the road, jacked up, the driver changing a tire. Eden gripped the seat with tense fingers. Things could be worse: she could be the passenger whose taxi had the flat tire.

They arrived on David's street after midnight. Streetlights did little to relieve the gloom. The taxi pulled to a stop, and Eden peered through the rain-streaked car window, immediately reminded of another rainy night that she had sat outside this house. It had looked beckoning then.

Now it seemed dark and uninviting. She glanced again at the streetlight. The power wasn't off. Why weren't the lights on inside the house? Her bad feeling doubled. Where was David? He should have been here long before her. Was it his cab on the freeway?

"You gettin' out, lady, or you want to go back to the hotel?"

"Getting out. But I want you to wait." She gathered her courage and raced through the rain to the porch. She lifted her hand to the door, but the moment her knuckles connected with it, it swung open. Her nerves leapt. "David?"

Her voice echoed eerily in the house, as if the whole place were devoid of people. Fixtures. Furniture. Life. With her heart in her throat, she stepped into the foyer. "David?"

The silence brought her nightmare flooding into her mind again, the vision of his dead body uppermost. Striving to curb her fear, she forced herself to move into the house and, starting with the living room, she searched for him, turning on lights as she went from the living room to the kitchen, to the office, to the spare bedrooms.

The bathroom door hung open, and there was a smear of something dark red like fresh blood on the floor. She drew a sharp breath, retreating a step. Fear prickled her neck and tightened her skull. Was it David's blood? Would she find her nightmare had come true?

David's bedroom was at the end of the hall. She realized a light was on in there. She approached with caution. David's agonized voice cut through the stillness. "Eden!"

He was alive. She scrambled to the bedroom door and froze at the sight before her. David was kneeling, gripping a blood-soaked dagger. Again he spoke her name in that same agony-choked voice she'd heard a moment before.

But he wasn't speaking to her.

His cries were for the woman lying on the floor beside him, her face turned toward the wall. Her denim coat had a pool of dark liquid in the center of her back. Impossibly Eden felt she was looking at herself.

"David?" Her voice cracked.

He jerked as if he'd been struck by a whip.

He shifted toward her, lurching to his feet, rearing back in shock. His eyes were filled with tears, then disbelief and confusion. "Eden?"

His gaze flicked between Eden and the woman on the floor. "Then who?"

The front door crashed open, and footsteps clumped down the hall, coming closer. Eden lurched around.

A uniformed police officer appeared in the doorway, gun drawn. "Freeze."

Behind him, Kollecki materialized, his gun clutched in his beefy hand. "Put the knife down, Doc."

David shook his head, and Eden thought for a heart-stopping moment that the uniformed officer might shoot him. But David held the weapon up toward Kollecki. "It's not a knife. It's my letter opener."

"Put it down, Doc," Kollecki repeated more firmly.

David's body seemed to go limp. He dropped the letter opener to the floor, and the uniformed policeman lowered his gun and rushed forward, yanked David's arms behind him and began snapping on handcuffs.

Numb, Eden took a step toward David, but Kollecki motioned her back, then went to check on the woman on the floor. "Too late for this one. Read him the *Miranda,* Joe. Even though we've caught him dead to rights, I want everything done by the book this time."

With that, Kollecki, who'd been a one-man task force set on making her life a living hell, smiled down at her as if they were old friends. "Good thing you called me, Mrs. Prescott. Love sure is blind. Be glad you wised up in time. He didn't hurt you, did he?"

Chapter Sixteen

"You called Kollecki?" David sounded stunned, hurt.

Eden cringed inside. "Yes. But I . . . David, I swear I only called him because I was afraid for you."

Traces of shock still hovered in his mossy eyes. He did believe her, didn't he?

"Quit wasting your time on this guy." Kollecki stepped between them and pointed to the body on the floor. "Don't you get it? He killed this woman thinking he was killing you."

Eden felt shock pulling the heat from her body. She had no doubt Kollecki was half-right—this woman had been killed because someone thought it was her. But David wasn't that someone.

Kollecki's accusation had a more violent effect on David. He shouted, "No! I didn't kill anyone. I was in the bathroom looking through the drawers."

Kollecki rolled his eyes. "For what?"

David's forehead furrowed as if he were trying to recall something. A long moment passed before it smoothed. "Combs."

"Combs? Hah!" Kollecki shook his head and glanced at the uniformed policeman. "Couldn't make up his mind if he wanted to stab the woman or comb her hair. Now I've heard everything."

David scowled at Kollecki but didn't expound on his search for the combs. "I heard the board in the hall creak. It does that if someone steps on it. Before I could investigate, something slammed against the back of my head. Knocked me out, I guess. You can feel the lump if you don't believe me."

Kollecki made no attempt to do so. "How long were you out?"

"I don't know. When I came to, I was holding the letter opener. There was blood on my shirt and hands." He glanced down at his stomach, at the dark splotches despoiling his shirtfront, swallowed hard, then raised his eyes again to Kollecki. "At first I thought I'd sustained a cut of some kind, but I couldn't find a wound. Then I realized whoever had hit me might still be in the house. I staggered in here to use the telephone and found…her." He shuddered. "I thought it was Eden."

Eden could see Kollecki didn't believe David. She knew exactly how tenacious the detective could be, how he could use the truth against his suspects. "Don't say another word. Not without a lawyer."

David glanced at her, then back at the body. He shuddered again, but the color was returning to his face, the shock subsiding. "Who is she?"

"You don't know?" Kollecki asked.

David shook his head. Kollecki glanced at Eden. "You know?"

Eden glanced again at the woman on the floor. "No. I can't see her face from this angle."

Kollecki leaned over the woman and, without touching anything, studied what he could see of her face. The tension in the room was punctuated by his silence. At length, the detective said, "Well, I'll be damned."

He straightened and grinned at David. "Unless I miss my guess, it's the woman you came here to meet tonight, Doc."

"Rose Hatcher?" David blanched. "But her hair is waist length. Red."

"Well, apparently to keep from being captured and returned to prison, she whacked it off and dyed it black."

Rose Hatcher. Eden's stomach lurched. The irony of this made her sick. *Rose's attempts to hide her identity had inadvertently contributed to her own murder.* Eden began to shake.

Another uniformed police officer entered the room. "The M.E. and his crew are on their way."

"Good." Kollecki's cheeks were puffed and red. "The doc's going to lockup. Mrs. Prescott, can one of my men give you a lift somewhere?"

"No. I have a taxi waiting." Eden glanced uncertainly at David. "Are you taking David to Issaquah?"

"Yeah, but don't waste your time following. You won't be able to see him."

Concern filled David's eyes. "He's right, Eden. Please go back to the hotel. Keep the doors locked. You'll be safe there...and the hospital might call about Beth. I'll join you as soon as my lawyer secures bail."

Kollecki chuckled at that. "Don't expect the doctor anytime tonight, ma'am."

EDEN REFUSED to answer the curious taxi driver's questions on the ride back to the hotel. Stiffly she stared out the window, feeling as flat and lifeless as the fine drizzle now coating the streets. Eventually the driver took the hint, and the rest of the ride was made in silence.

Still reeling, Eden entered the hotel lobby, feeling like a wraith stumbling aimlessly through the graveyard that her life had become. She checked the desk for messages and was grateful that on this night of horrors, no one had called to say Beth's body was rejecting the new kidney. So far, her sister was alive and well.

It was more than could be said for Rose Hatcher.

Eden waited for an elevator. Had Rose been framed for Marianne DePaul's murder? Had she been just another pawn in the stalker's cat-and-mouse game? If so, she might have died no matter what Eden or David could have done to prevent it. Eden stepped onto the elevator. What was the truth? Was Rose murdered because of what she'd known or because she'd resembled Eden from the back?

Eden trembled. Instinctively she knew it was the latter. Cold seemed to seep from her pores, chilling every inch of her, bringing on an overwhelming fear. *She* was meant to have died on David's bedroom floor tonight—with David framed for her murder. The stalker's obsession had taken a macabre turn from fixated love to malevolent hatred.

The suite no longer seemed like an elegant love nest. Just an expensive prison. She was exhausted. Wiped out. Dizzy. Even though she didn't expect to sleep, Eden crawled into bed with her clothes on. But she did sleep, long and restless hours.

The telephone woke her. Groggily she opened her eyes to the gray daylight spilling through the room. The phone rang again, and her pulse revved. Was it the hospital? News of David? She all but shouted an anxious "Hello?"

It was David's lawyer.

"How is he?"

"Tired." The man had a bass voice that conjured an image of someone middle-aged, tall and snowy haired. In reality, he was in his thirties, short and balding. "Detective Kollecki's been questioning him all night. You should know, he's determined to pin this on my client."

Eden's heart sank. She sat up. Finding herself slightly light-headed, she eased back onto the pillows and shut her eyes, trying to find reasons to counter Kollecki's dogged determination to railroad David. Her eyes came open as a memory rushed back. "But he was hit over the head. Surely a doctor will confirm that."

"Already has, but Detective Kollecki's claiming the wound was self-inflicted. After the search his men did of Dr. Coulter's house, he thinks he has a rock-solid case."

Disquiet twisted her stomach into a knot. "What did they find?"

"White rose petals in his refrigerator. A white rosebush in his backyard. A green shirt Dr. Coulter claims was stolen." He spoke as if he was ticking the items off a list. "The shirt's covered with dried bloodstains that Detective Kollecki seems to think will tie Dr. Coulter to another of his unsolved murders."

"Whose?"

"I'm not sure...but your former sister-in-law's name came up once or twice."

"Val?" Her throat was so dry she couldn't swallow. Kollecki could accuse David all he wanted, could find a whole greenhouse full of white roses in David's basement, but she'd never believe for one minute that he could kill anyone. "Why? What reason does Kollecki give for David killing Valerie? Or Rose Hatcher? Or any of the other victims, for that matter?''

"That's our ace in the hole. My client has no motive in this or any of the detective's cases." He paused. "Try not to worry. So far, they're only questioning Dr. Coulter. He hasn't been booked. The forensics team is still at his house. Maybe they'll turn up something that will point to the real murderer. I'll call you later when I know more."

Eden decided to call the hospital to check on Beth. Denise Smalley's voice rang familiarly in her ear. "Fourth floor. Transplant wing."

Eden considered hanging up, then realized it would gain her nothing. She'd have to call back and she'd still have to talk to Denise. "This is Eden Prescott."

She heard a sharp intake of breath...as if Denise hadn't expected to speak to her again...ever. "You!"

"Yes, me." Eden swallowed hard. *Had* Denise thought she was dead? "May I speak to my sister's nurse?"

After a weighted pause, Denise said, "I'll see if she's available."

There was a click on the line, and music filled Eden's ear. A minute passed. Three minutes. Five. Seven. She reached to press down the disconnect button but was stopped by a voice issuing through the phone. "Hello, Mrs. Prescott."

Eden resettled the telephone to her ear. "How is Beth doing?"

"Her signs are good. No indication of rejection so far, but it's early days," she cautioned.

Relief skittered through Eden. But the nurse's warning about "early days" could not be dismissed. Right now they had to take it hour by hour. It was dangerous to build unrealistic expectations. At this point, rejection could occur at any time. But on a day when so much seemed desolate, she couldn't help grasping the tiny thread of hope. "Please tell Beth I'll be in in about an hour."

Eden stood. Dizziness attacked, dropping her back onto the bed. She drew several deep breaths, but starting at the corners of her eyes, a curtain of black seemed to be slowly drawing together. She lowered her head between her knees.

The curtain ebbed away, and soon the room came sharply back in focus. She gave herself another five minutes, then stood again. All light-headedness had gone. She showered, dressed, then took a cab to the university medical center.

Her mind was on David. She knew exactly how he had to be feeling—trapped by Kollecki's unyielding tenacity. She had desperately wanted Shannon and Peter's murderer to be found, to absolve her, to restore her reputation. Neither had predicted the murderer would turn the tables on them, that her vindication would cost David his freedom. His life.

The black thought lost some of its terror in the knowledge that the forensics team was still searching David's house. There was hope that something would be found to clear him. It would even be sweet justice if that something made Kollecki eat crow. The idea strengthened her, and she arrived at the medical center heartened.

The lobby corridor held the expected swarm of activity, visitors and personnel flitting to and fro. The tantalizing aroma of espresso slowed her steps. She glanced longingly toward the cart set in the solarium. Wasn't caffeine bad for pregnant women? She'd have to ask her doctor before she indulged in any of her favorite double *lattes*.

She was about to turn away when she spotted Lynzy at one of the solarium tables. She was alone. Eden hesitated. Should she tell her about David, or leave that up to him? *And let Lynzy find out from a news broadcast, or from someone who'd heard a news broadcast?* Better that she tell Lynzy instead.

Lynzy's brown eyes widened, and a warm smile parted her lips as Eden asked if she could join her for a few minutes. "Sure. Sit down. How's your sister?"

"Fine."

"Don't you want some espresso?"

"Not now, thank you." Eden didn't know how to begin. She glanced around to make certain they wouldn't be overheard. No one sat near enough for that. Still, she leaned closer and lowered her voice. "I feel I ought to tell you what has happened so you will be able to handle things if it becomes necessary."

"What kind of things?" Lynzy peered over the top of her cup. "You look like it must be something pretty harsh."

"Harsh. Yes, you could call it that. Rose Hatcher was murdered last night at Dr. Coulter's house."

Lynzy gasped, then blushed crimson, obviously embarrassed by the loudness of her response. "Sorry. Oh, not that she's dead. I'm glad. I've been scared silly since Doc said she'd escaped from jail. Who killed her?"

"We don't know. But the police have David in for questioning, and it looks as if they may charge him."

"What? No way." Lynzy shook her head like a stubborn child. "Doc wouldn't off anybody."

"We know that. Let's just hope there's some proof."
Eden drew a shaky breath. "Lynzy, promise me you'll
keep this under your hat. Don't tell anyone."

"Not even Colleen?"

Eden sat back. Lynzy was the only suspect on their
list she trusted. But if Colleen wasn't the murderer, she
also had the right to be told privately about David. "Is
she coming in today?"

"No. She left a message that she was going to spend
the day with her mother."

"Then let's do this. If anyone asks you about David
being arrested or at the police station, then try and reach
Colleen and tell her. Otherwise, it's our secret.
Agreed?"

"You betcha."

"I have to see my sister now." Eden stood.

"Keep me posted—on Doc and on Beth, okay?"

"Of course."

With her mind on David, Eden headed down the hall
toward the elevators. Alone in the crowd of people, she
felt vulnerable, jumpy, fearful. Someone had meant to
murder her last night. *She'll have quite a shock when
she discovers I'm still alive.* Eden thought again of
Denise's stunned voice when she'd identified herself.
She tensed. Maybe the stalker already knew.

She squeezed into the elevator, her discomfort hugging her like a cloak. Could she reach Beth's room
without seeing Denise? The security guard would be
there. The thought of him buoyed her. But as the elevator doors slipped open, she realized Denise would
probably be at the desk. Fear shivered through her. She
couldn't get to Beth's room quick enough.

Several people exited the elevator with her. She turned
toward the transplant wing. Out of the corner of her

eye, she saw a woman lurch out of one of the waiting-area chairs and rush toward her as if she'd been waiting for the elevator.

Eden focused on the nurses' station ahead. Denise was there. Her gaze drilled into Eden, and even from this distance, Eden could see she'd been waiting for her.

Her mouth went dry, and her steps faltered. Denise was rounding the end of the counter, coming toward her.

"Eden?" From behind her, a woman's voice sounded close to her ear, stopping Eden cold.

She turned around and glanced into the familiar face, surprise darting through her. "What are you doing here?"

"THIS LITTLE SWATCH of cloth doesn't prove a thing, Doc." Kollecki stopped pacing and dangled a tiny plastic bag at David. "If Tagg can't find anything at her house to verify your story, you're going down for the murders of Rose Hatcher, Shannon Smalley and Peter and Valerie Prescott."

They were in Kollecki's office—had been since the forensics team had found that bit of fabric under Rose Hatcher's body this morning. David watched the swinging plastic bag as if it were a pendant held by a hypnotist. His freedom depended on that bit of cloth. His life. Eden's life. But Kollecki refused to warn Eden until they had proof of the woman's guilt. "This waiting is hell."

"We'll hear soon." His lawyer spoke from his spot in a chair against the wall.

"Even if you're right about this woman," Kollecki continued, "I might charge you with harboring a fugitive."

David's head jerked up. "Harboring a fugitive?"

Kollecki's little black eyes were hot with impatience. Waiting wasn't his strong suit. "Suppressing information about an escaped convict's whereabouts—it's the same thing."

"I called and left a message for Detective Tagg. He didn't call me back."

"He wasn't on duty. Why didn't you ask for me?"

David clamped his mouth shut. If he told the truth about that, it would only prejudice Kollecki against him all the more.

The lawyer said, "How did Miss Hatcher get into Dr. Coulter's house?"

Kollecki stopped his pacing and lurched around. "We found a broken window in the basement."

"Tell Tagg to look for a key to my front door," David interjected. "It has to be how the other woman got in to take my combs, my green polo shirt and the letter opener."

"If Tagg finds anything at all, I'll be sure he checks for that, too."

The phone rang, sending David's heart into his throat. He sat on the edge of his seat. Kollecki answered and assured them it was Detective Tagg.

Even hearing only one side of the conversation, it was obvious that they had the stalker.

David's body flushed cold, then hot. He leapt from his chair, panic scurrying through him. "We need to warn Eden."

Kollecki signaled for him to use Tagg's phone on the opposite desk.

David called the hotel first, and as the clerk informed him Eden had left for the hospital, his gaze fell on the scrap of fabric in the tiny plastic bag. As he'd known the moment he'd seen it, the hot-pink rayon could only have come from one of Ariel Bell's uniforms.

With anxiety prickling him, he called the transplant wing and told Denise to have Eden call him on his cell phone the moment she came in. Then he phoned Lynzy.

"Kollecki!" David slammed the phone down. "We've got to get to the hospital! My student assistant said she spoke with Eden over half an hour ago. Eden told her she was going straight up to see her sister, but the desk nurse claims she never showed up. What if she ran into Ariel?"

"THE QUESTION IS, what are *you* doing still alive?" Ariel's hand was in her pocket. "I've got a gun in here. It's little but it would make a nice hole in you."

The heat drained from Eden's body, and she realized she probably resembled the ghost Ariel had thought she was.

"Mrs. Prescott." Denise Smalley's voice brought Eden jerking around, grasping at the chance of rescue.

Denise was some twenty feet away. Eden took a step toward her, but Ariel snatched her by the upper arm, jerking her back. Eden felt herself slam against Ariel's side, felt the hard barrel of the gun pressing her ribs.

Ariel whispered, "One word and I'll use this."

Eden doubted Ariel would do that . . . with Denise as a witness. But she knew if she cried out for help, Ariel was unstable enough, unpredictable enough, to do anything. Eden wouldn't risk endangering others' lives.

Denise stopped ten feet from them. A puzzled look crossed her face, but before she asked the question hovering on her lips, Ariel said, "It's okay, Denise. I told her."

"Good." Denise retreated as if she'd been spared a distasteful chore.

Eden's heart sank to her toes.

"Come on. We're going for a walk." Ariel pivoted again, dragging Eden with her.

Scrambling to think of some way out of this predicament, Eden offered no resistance. Like someone holding up an elderly patient, Ariel steered her into the hall away from the transplant wing until they reached the elevators to the BB Tower—the slowest elevators in the state of Washington.

As the doors lurched closed behind them, Eden felt Ariel's grip on her slacken.

Eden peered up at her. "What did Denise think you told me?"

Ariel's grin was nasty. "They've been trying to reach you at the hotel. Beth's body is rejecting the kidney."

Eden jerked as if the words were a fist smacking her. Dizziness wobbled her equilibrium.

"None of that!" Ariel jerked her up, fingers biting into Eden's arms. She was strong—likely from handling patients, likely from a strain of madness.

I won't think of Beth. Not now. If I do, I might die . . . and then my baby will die. So help her God, she would do everything within her power to prevent that. But how?

The elevator slipped past the fifth floor. The sixth. Hadn't she read somewhere that murderers liked to boast about their feats? Maybe she could buy some thinking time by getting Ariel talking. "You've loved David a long time, haven't you?"

She felt Ariel stiffen, but she remained tight-mouthed. Eden guessed she had no intention of answering. The elevator rose past the ninth floor. Eden scrambled for another tack.

"Ever since I worked with his brother's daughter." Ariel's voice slipped out so softly it was nearly inaudible.

The elevator passed the eleventh floor. Eden swallowed hard. If she said the wrong thing, it might set Ariel off. She chose her words carefully. "What attracted you to him?"

"He was the kindest man I'd ever met."

Eden watched the lighted board illuminate floor thirteen. Then fourteen.

"He looked at me when he talked to me, you know, really looked *at* me, as if he actually saw me. Not like most men. They're only after the package, not the woman inside."

"You're right. David isn't that kind of man."

The elevator ground to a halt. The sixteenth floor. Ariel gazed down at Eden, her gray eyes hard, flat stones. "You'd know that better than I, wouldn't you?"

The elevator doors joggled open.

Eden cringed, her stomach writhing with fear. David was the wrong subject. She needed to steer clear of Ariel's defeats, concentrate on what she probably considered her successes.

"Why did you kill Shannon?" Eden dropped the question like a bomb. Ariel tensed and glared at her. Then, as the elevator doors started closing, she hustled Eden out onto the sixteenth floor.

She steered her left, then left again, and Eden realized they were going to David's office. Why? If Ariel intended to shoot her here, it wouldn't be to frame him for another murder; David was still in custody. A damp

chill brushed her skin. She couldn't afford to waste time
trying to figure out Ariel's motives for anything.

Just keep her talking. Eden struggled to recall what
she'd asked. Oh, yes. Shannon. "Why did you kill her?
She had no romantic ties to David."

"I feel bad about that." Ariel grimaced, but if she
actually felt remorseful, it didn't show. "Denise is my
friend. But it's her own fault. She thought Shannon had
the hots for David. I knew they spent time together, but
he didn't seem enamored of her the way Denise claimed.
Then Denise told me she'd caught Shannon reading
bridal magazines. I wasn't about to let the little twit take
David from me."

She said this as if she believed David and she had
some kind of special commitment. If she weren't so
frightened, Eden might have felt sorry for this woman.
They passed one office, then another and another. It
was lunchtime, and the corridor was deserted. "Surely
you realized your mistake when you found her with Peter?"

"Well, that little joke was on me." She laughed hu-
morlessly. "I thought Shannon was alone. When he
came out of the bathroom and found me standing over
her body—let's just say he scared me as badly as I
scared him." She laughed again. "Actually I'd say I
scared him worse."

Eden shoved the awful visions out of her mind. They
stopped outside David's office. Ariel tried the knob.
Would Lynzy be there? Eden prayed not. She didn't
want the nice young woman harmed. The door was
locked.

Eden's relief was short-lived, as Ariel produced a set
of keys from her pocket and unlocked it. She shoved

Eden inside, relocked the door, then forced Eden through the first office and into David's private one.

The door banged eerily behind them, and desolation settled around Eden with ugly inevitability, as gray as the clouds outside. She scanned the desk and bookshelves for something to use as a weapon. Her knees were wobbly. She spotted a paperweight on the corner of the desk farthest from the windows. Could she reach it?

Ariel brought the gun out of her pocket and pointed it at her stomach. "Get over by the windows."

Shrinking away from the gun barrel, Eden walked backward until she bumped against the heating unit below the windows. She'd never reach the paperweight from here. Panic slithered through her.

Out of the corner of her eye, she spied the jade plant on top of the heater. It was in a weighty-looking ceramic container. Could she divert Ariel's attention enough to heft it? "What was Valerie's crime?"

"If you must know, she saw me following you. Asked me about it when I went to pick up my check. I couldn't have her telling anyone." Keeping the gun leveled at her, Ariel moved around David's desk and rummaged through the top drawer. She lifted out a pair of sharp-tipped scissors, then moved toward Eden like a panther stalking her prey.

Eden blanched, eyeing the scissors uncertainly. What did she mean to do with them? "Did you frame Rose Hatcher?"

That stopped Ariel. With the hand holding the scissors, she ruffled her wild hair and beamed with pride. "I went to a lot of trouble befriending that timid mouse. Then I just left a few incriminating items in her apartment."

Her gray eyes suddenly narrowed into slits. "That sneaky Marianne DePaul. She meant to steal David away from me. She was always hanging around his office, eating in the lunchroom with him, calling him at his brother James's house."

She glared at Eden. "But you—you were the worst."

Eden chose that moment to charge the bigger, taller Ariel. She slammed into her with all her might. Her attack was as effective as a gnat hitting a cockroach. And it incensed Ariel further.

She dropped the scissors, grabbed Eden by the forearm and jammed the gun against her belly.

"No. Please. I'm going to have a baby."

Ariel's eyes flashed with hatred. Eden realized she'd made a mistake mentioning the baby. Ariel shoved her back against the heating unit, then bent to retrieve the scissors. Eden crossed her hands protectively over her stomach.

Ariel thrust her body against Eden's, jammed Eden against the heating unit, holding her there while she reached over Eden's head and poked the scissor tip into the tiny, square window lock. A special key was required to open the windows on this floor, a key kept by security. To Eden's horror, the scissors worked just as effectively. The window swung open.

Cold stole into the office, cutting through Eden's clothes. Ariel stepped back, and Eden slumped, grabbing in a lungful of much-needed air. The gun barrel was pushed into her face, and Ariel pointed to the top of the heating unit. "Up you go."

Eden shook her head.

"Now." Ariel thumbed the hammer.

Eden froze. "Please don't kill me."

"I'm not going to kill you. You're going to commit suicide."

"No one will believe that."

"Yes, they will. Your life is a shambles. Everyone thinks you killed your husband and his lover. You're pregnant with the baby of a man who will hang for murdering—" Ariel broke off, tilting her head. "Who *did* I stab last night?"

Eden let out a ragged breath. "Rose Hatcher."

"Rose?" Ariel shrieked with laughter. "That's rich. What was she doing at David's?"

"She was going to tell David about you. I think she saw you put the rose on his porch after you killed Valerie."

"Serves her right, then." She chortled. "I can't wait to see tomorrow's headlines. Former suspect throws herself out lover's office window after learning he's a killer, after learning her sister's kidney transplant fails."

She jabbed the gun in Eden's ribs. "Now, get on the heater."

Unless she could reach one of the jade plants and hit Ariel with it, she was going to die. Eden had never been more sure of anything in her life. "I can't get up there without a chair."

"Then drag one over."

Eden stepped to the high-backed leather chair, grasped the arms and tugged. Despite the fact she was holding something solid, her balance wavered. She swayed, then lost her grip. The black curtain she'd experienced earlier that morning slid across her eyes.

Eden crumpled at Ariel's feet.

Ariel swore. Then she decided an unconscious Eden was preferable to a conscious one: no more arguing, no fighting and no screaming. She set her gun down, squatted and scooped Eden up like an unwieldy grocery sack. As petite as she was, Eden's deadweight was an armful.

Grunting, Ariel straightened and staggered toward the window. The outer office door creaked. Then the door at her back banged open, galvanizing her.

Kollecki shouted, "Freeze, Ms. Bell!"

Ariel didn't even glance over her shoulder.

Kollecki said, "Turn around, real slow, and put Mrs. Prescott down."

Ariel stood stiff with defiance.

David stepped into his office. His gaze was riveted on what he could see of Eden. What had happened to her? He spotted the gun on the floor. Had Ariel shot her? Fear raced his heart. But he knew any quick movements might set Ariel off.

"Please, Ariel. Don't hurt her." David didn't know what else to say. Before Ariel had tried framing him for murder, he'd have used her affection for him to reason with her. Now she hated him. Nothing he said would convince her to trust him.

Kollecki repeated his command that Ariel turn around and put Eden down.

"The only place I'm putting her is out this window." Ariel took a step forward.

Kollecki shot her in the knee.

The bang resounded in the confined space. Ariel screamed and crumpled backward, tossing Eden free as she fell. Eden's head cracked against the desk. David ran to her. She was breathing. But a lump was forming at her temple, and he couldn't get her to wake up.

Chapter Seventeen

Light prodded Eden awake. Carnations scented the air, and it took her a moment to realize she was not in a garden but a hospital bed. Her gaze focused on a beloved face, and she smiled. The effort hurt. "David..."

He breathed a sigh of relief. "It's so great to see those gorgeous eyes of yours."

"Thank you for the flowers." Dozens of red carnations seemed to occupy every available space in the room.

"They're from Kollecki. It's probably the only apology we can expect from him."

Agreeing that his assessment of the detective was right on, Eden smiled wryly. "Thank God he had the sensibility not to send white roses."

"More likely roses just cost too much." David smirked, then leaned over her. "How are you feeling, love?"

She winced. "My head hurts like the devil."

"Slight concussion." He lifted her hand and kissed the palm. "It happened when Ariel dropped you. But the doctor assures me you'll be up and around by tomorrow."

Fear flushed through her at the sudden rush of memory brought to life with that one name. She gripped his hand. "Ariel?"

"Down the hall. Under arrest. Kollecki shot her in the knee."

Eden shuddered and sank back on the pillow. She closed her eyes. Then, as the pain eased, she looked again into the eyes of the man she loved. "Ariel told me everything. She killed them all."

"I know. The police searched her house and car and turned up enough evidence to put her away for several lifetimes." He kissed her forehead. "So I don't want you wasting one more minute worrying about her."

Ariel was a worry Eden gladly relinquished, but her sister's failed kidney surgery was utmost in her thoughts. Her throat was dry, her tongue thick. "Beth?"

David grinned. "Beth is great. The kidney is functioning as well as if it were an original piece of her anatomy."

Had she heard him right? Yes. He was grinning. The icy cloak around her heart shattered, and a joyful sob spilled from her. "Ariel said her body was rejecting the kidney."

"Ah, love." His look of sympathy said more than words. "She lied. Dr. Ingalls says it is an incredibly good match. She's already starting to heal."

Tears of relief and happiness sprang into Eden's eyes, wetting her lashes. She swept her hands from her chin up to her eyes and felt a lump in the general area of her right temple. Pain spiraled through her head at the gentle brushing of her fingers over it. "How did I get this?"

David edged onto the bed and braced his arms on each side of her body. He told her as much as he knew of the events. "You were unconscious when I arrived. Did Ariel hit you with something?"

"I fainted." Eden blanched, recalling with a brand-new fear why she had fainted. Had Ariel dropping her harmed her baby? She placed her hands over her stomach. "David, did the doctor check? Is...everything else okay?"

He sighed, then sat straighter and placed his hands over hers. "If you're asking about this little baby...yes, everything else is perfect."

He knew. Eden's heart climbed her throat. "The doctor told you?"

He nodded. His mouth stretched into a thin line. "Why didn't you tell me about our baby, Eden?"

Eden's pulse tripped at his assumption that the baby was theirs. How could she tell him she didn't know who the baby's father was? Would he hate her? Reject her?

Steeling herself, she spoke softly. "I knew I couldn't keep it from you much longer." Somehow she managed to sound more calm than she felt. "But I had two reasons for waiting. First, you have to know that I'd never use a child to trap you into a lifelong commitment you didn't want. And second, you also need to know...this baby might be Peter's."

She saw the shock register, then he grew thoughtful. His eyes changed from mossy to jade. "What if the baby is mine?"

She could barely breathe. "If he or she proves to be yours, I'll make certain you have a part in your child's life...if that's what you want."

"Do you love me, Eden?"

Did she love him? How could he even ask? She feathered her fingers along his strong jaw. "Enough to let you go...if that's what you want."

He threw back his head and drew in a long breath. Letting it out slowly, he sought her gaze. "I thought you didn't want the commitment...so soon after being widowed, so soon after coming out of a bad marriage...so I didn't ask you to make any promises that would burden you."

He kissed her fingertips. "But me...I want to spend the rest of my life with you and raise as big a family as we can together."

Gently he placed his palm over her belly again, his gaze hot with the passion of his words. "I don't give a damn about biology. I already know who the father of this baby is...me. Is that what you want?"

Despite the ache in her head, she grinned with all the wonder and hope and love that were filling her heart. "That is definitely what I want. For me and for *our* baby."

HARLEQUIN®

INTRIGUE®

COMING NEXT MONTH

#385 BULLETPROOF HEART by Sheryl Lynn
Lawman
Reb Tremaine appeared on the Double Bar R, his sexy lips saying
he could handle horses and his eyes saying maybe he could love a
widow like Emily Farraday. But Emily was in trouble. And the
danger didn't stop when she realized that everything Reb had told
her about himself was lies....

#386 TELL ME NO LIES by Patricia Rosemoor
The McKenna Legacy
Rosalind Van Straatan needed to know the truth about the night her
legendary grandmother confessed to a murder she probably didn't
commit. The irreverent and disturbingly sexy Skelly McKenna wasn't
exactly her first choice of investigative partners; unfortunately, he was
her only choice.

#387 SPENCER'S SHADOW by Laura Gordon
The Spencer Brothers
Anne Osborne desperately needed a hero, but Cole Spencer didn't
agree with his brother that he was the best man for the job. But then he
gazed into Anne's trusting eyes, and he knew he'd go to the ends of
the earth to protect this classy lady from a ruthless killer who thought
Anne knew too much.

#388 A BABY'S CRY by Amanda Stevens
Ten years after Dillon Reeves walked out on her, Taylor Robinson had
reason to believe that their child was not stillborn, as she'd been told.
Dillon had never known about the pregnancy, but would he agree to
help Taylor find their child?

AVAILABLE THIS MONTH:

Look for us on-line at: http://www.romance.net

MILLION DOLLAR SWEEPSTAKES

SWP-M96

REBECCA
43 LIGHT STREET
YORK
FACE TO FACE

*Bestselling author Rebecca York returns to "43 Light Street"
for an original story of past secrets, deadly deceptions—and
the most intimate betrayal.*

She woke in a hospital—with amnesia...and with child.
According to her rescuer, whose striking face is the last
image she remembers, she's Justine Hollingsworth. But
nothing about her life seems to fit, except for the baby
inside her and Mike Lancer's arms around her. Consumed
by forbidden passion and racked by nameless fear, she
must discover if she is Justine...or the victim of some mind
game. Her life—and her unborn child's—depends on it....

Don't miss *Face To Face*—Available in October, wherever
Harlequin books are sold.

HARLEQUIN ®

®

43FTF

HARLEQUIN®

INTRIGUE®

The Spencer Brothers—Cole and Drew...
two tough hombres.

Meet

Cole Spencer
Somehow this cowboy found himself playing bodyguard.
But the stunningly lovely, maddeningly independent
Anne Osborne would just as soon string him up as let
him get near her body.

#387 SPENCER'S SHADOW
September 1996

Drew Spencer
He was a P.I. on a mission. When Joanna Caldwell-
Galbraith sought his help in finding her missing
husband—dead or alive—Drew knew this was his
chance. He'd lost Joanna once to that scoundrel...he
wouldn't lose her again.

#396 SPENCER'S BRIDE
November 1996

The Spencer Brothers—they're just what you need to
warm you up on a crisp fall night!

TSB

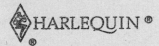

HARLEQUIN®

I N T R I G U E®

> *To my darling grandchildren,*
> *I leave you my love and more. Within thirty-three*
> *days of your thirty-third birthday you will have in*
> *your grasp a legacy of which your dreams are made.*
> *Dreams are not always tangible things, but more*
> *often are born in the heart. Act selflessly in another's*
> *behalf, and my legacy shall be yours.*
>
> *Your loving grandmother,*
> *Moira McKenna*

You are cordially invited to the McKenna Family
Reunion! Share in the legacy of a lifetime
as only Patricia Rosemoor—and
Harlequin Intrigue —can deliver.

The McKenna clan—some are good, some are evil.... If
the good prevail, there will be a family reunion. Find out
in the exciting McKenna Legacy trilogy:

#382 SEE ME IN YOUR DREAMS
#386 TELL ME NO LIES
#390 TOUCH ME IN THE DARK

Coming in August, September and October from
Patricia Rosemoor and Harlequin Intrigue.
Don't miss any of them!

Free Gift Offer

With a Free Gift proof-of-purchase
from any Harlequin® book, you can receive
a beautiful cubic zirconia pendant.

This stunning marquise-shaped stone is a genuine cubic
zirconia—accented by an 18" gold tone necklace.
(Approximate retail value $19.95)

Send for yours today...
compliments of ◆HARLEQUIN®

To receive your free gift, a cubic zirconia pendant, send us one original proof-of-purchase, photocopies not accepted, from the back of any Harlequin Romance®, Harlequin Presents®, Harlequin Temptation®, Harlequin Superromance®, Harlequin Intrigue®, Harlequin American Romance®, or Harlequin Historicals® title available in August, September or October at your favorite retail outlet, together with the Free Gift Certificate, plus a check or money order for $1.65 U.S./$2.15 CAN. (do not send cash) to cover postage and handling, payable to Harlequin Free Gift Offer. We will send you the specified gift. Allow 6 to 8 weeks for delivery. Offer good until October 31, 1996 or while quantities last. Offer valid in the U.S. and Canada only.

Free Gift Certificate

Name: _____

Address: _____

City: _____ State/Province: _____ Zip/Postal Code: _____

Mail this certificate, one proof-of-purchase and a check or money order for postage and handling to: HARLEQUIN FREE GIFT OFFER 1996. In the U.S.: 3010 Walden Avenue, P.O. Box 9071, Buffalo NY 14269-9057. In Canada: P.O. Box 604, Fort Erie, Ontario L2Z 5X3.

FREE GIFT OFFER   084-KMF
ONE PROOF-OF-PURCHASE
To collect your fabulous FREE GIFT, a cubic zirconia pendant, you must include this original proof-of-purchase for each gift with the properly completed Free Gift Certificate.

084-KMF

You're About to Become a *Privileged Woman*

Reap the rewards of fabulous free gifts and benefits with proofs-of-purchase from Harlequin and Silhouette books

Pages & Privileges™

It's our way of thanking you for buying our books at your favorite retail stores.

Pages & Privileges™

Harlequin and Silhouette— the most privileged readers in the world!

For more information about Harlequin and Silhouette's PAGES & PRIVILEGES program call the Pages & Privileges Benefits Desk: 1-503-794-2499

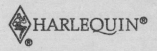

HARLEQUIN®

HI-PP167